"When Your Father Introduced Us, You Thought I Was Coming On To You?"

Well, she had. But Colin looked so insulted, so genuinely appalled by the accusation, now she wasn't so sure.

"It wouldn't be the first time," she said, but she was losing steam, and the excuse sounded hollow. Was she so jaded, so warped from past experiences that she would misinterpret the most innocent of gestures? Could she no longer trust her own instincts? And if she couldn't trust herself, who could she trust?

"Your father did mention that you've had problems in the past with unscrupulous men."

Rowena's father didn't even know the half of it. "I guess it's made me a little paranoid. Which I know is a terrible excuse."

"If I came on too strong, I apologize." He paused. "That happens sometimes when I meet a beautiful woman."

Dear Reader,

My husband and I have something that we like to call "Mole Stories." I know that probably sounds a little strange, so let me explain.

After twenty-four years of marriage, you would think that a person would have learned all there is to know about their spouse. So this one day I'm looking at my husband's chin, and I ask, "Didn't you used to have a mole there?" Bear in mind that through the course of our marriage he's usually had either a full beard or goatee, so it's not *too* weird that I'm just noticing this now. He explains that yes, he did have a mole. It just appeared out of nowhere when he was a kid—completely freaking out his parents, of course. After thorough examination it was determined to be harmless, and they were told to "keep an eye on it." Eventually it started to fade, and now it's gone.

As he's telling me this story I realize this is something about the man I had spent the past twenty-four-plus years with that I had never known before. Hence the "mole story" was born. Now every time one of us tells the other something we hadn't heard before, it is automatically referred to as a Mole Story.

Which has nothing to do with the book, but it's kind of a cool story on its own.

Until next time,

Michelle

MICHELLE CELMER

BEDROOM DIPLOMACY

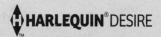

HARLEQUIN® DESIRE

Special thanks and acknowledgment to Michelle Celmer for her contribution to the Daughters of Power: The Capital miniseries.

Recycling programs
for this product may
not exist in your area.

ISBN-13: 978-0-373-73223-4

BEDROOM DIPLOMACY

Printed in U.S.A.

Books by Michelle Celmer

Harlequin Desire

Exposed: Her Undercover Millionaire #2084
†*One Month with the Magnate* #2099
†*A Clandestine Corporate Affair* #2106
†*Much More Than a Mistress* #2111
The Nanny Bombshell #2133
Princess in the Making #2175
§*Caroselli's Christmas Baby* #2194
Bedroom Diplomacy #2210

Silhouette Desire

The Secretary's Secret #1774
Best Man's Conquest #1799
**The King's Convenient Bride* #1876
**The Illegitimate Prince's Baby* #1877
**An Affair with the Princess* #1900
**The Duke's Boardroom Affair* #1919
Royal Seducer #1951
The Oilman's Baby Bargain #1970
**Christmas with the Prince* #1979
Money Man's Fiancée Negotiation #2006
**Virgin Princess, Tycoon's Temptation* #2026
**Expectant Princess, Unexpected Affair* #2032
†*The Tycoon's Paternity Agenda* #2053

Harlequin Superromance

Nanny Next Door #1685

Harlequin Special Edition

No Ordinary Joe #2196

Silhouette Special Edition

Accidentally Expecting #1847

†Black Gold Billionaires
*Royal Seductions
§The Caroselli Inheritance

Other titles by this author available in ebook format.

MICHELLE CELMER

is a bestselling author of more than thirty books. When she's not writing, she likes to spend time with her husband, kids, grandchildren and a menagerie of animals.

Michelle loves to hear from readers. Visit her website, www.michellecelmer.com, like her on Facebook or write her at P.O. Box 300, Clawson, MI 48017.

To Barb, Robbie, Rachel, Andrea and Jen.
It was a pleasure and a privilege working with you
on this project.

An enormous thank-you to my friend John
for sharing his military and piloting expertise,
and for the correspondence that helped to prevent me
from coming completely unglued during an
especially rigorous revision experience.

And finally to Steve, Josh and Alec, who tolerated
without complaint two weeks of fast food and PB&J, and
me roaming around in the wee hours like a zombie after
eighteen straight hours glued to the computer screen.

* * *

Daughters of Power: The Capital
*In a town filled with high-stakes players,
it's these women who really rule.*

Don't miss any of the books
in this scandalous new continuity
from Harlequin Desire!

A Conflict of Interest by Barbara Dunlop
Bedroom Diplomacy by Michelle Celmer
A Wedding She'll Never Forget by Robyn Grady
No Stranger to Scandal by Rachel Bailey
A Very *Exclusive Engagement* by Andrea Laurence
Affairs of State by Jennifer Lewis

One

Rowena Tate clung to what shred of patience she still possessed as her father's personal assistant, Margaret Wellington, warned her, "He said to tell you that he's on his way over now."

"And...?" Rowena said, knowing there was more.

"That's it," Margaret said, but Rowena could tell by her voice, the slight rise in pitch, that she was leaving something out.

"You're a worse liar than I am."

Margaret sighed, and in that sympathetic tone said, "He wanted me to remind you to be on your best behavior."

Rowena took a deep, calming breath. Her father had informed her by email this morning that he would be bringing a guest to see the day-care center. He'd demanded—not asked, because the great Senator Tate never asked for anything—that she have things in order. He'd suggested, not for the first time since she'd taken over the management of his pet project, that she was still impulsive, irresponsible and inept—labels that he apparently would never let her live down.

She looked out her office window at the children on the playground. Five straight days of rain had finally turned to sunny skies, and the temperature was a pleasant sixty-five degrees—about the norm for Southern California in February. Dressed in spring jackets, the day-care kids darted around, shaking off a severe case of cabin fever.

She could be in the world's worst mood, and watching the kids play always made her smile. Until she had her son, Dylan, she'd had little interest in children. Now she couldn't imagine a more satisfying career choice.

And she knew, if she wasn't careful, he would take that away from her, too.

"He's never going to trust me, is he?"

"He put you in charge."

"Yeah, but after three months he still watches me like a hawk. Sometimes I think he *wants* me to screw up, so he can say I told you so."

"He does not. He loves you, Row. He just doesn't know how to show it."

Having been her father's assistant for fifteen years, Margaret was like part of the family, and one of the few people who understood the complicated relationship between Rowena and her father. Margaret had been with them since before Rowena's mother, Amelia, caused an incredible scandal by taking off with the senator's protégé.

And people wondered why Rowena was so screwed up.

Was, she reminded herself. "Who is it this time?" she asked Margaret.

"A British diplomat. I don't know much about him, other than that he's lobbying your father to support a tech treaty with the U.K. And I think he has some sort of royal title."

The senator probably loved that. "Well, thanks for the heads-up."

"Good luck, honey."

The buzzer sounded, announcing her father's arrival. With a heavy sigh she pushed herself out of her chair, took off the paint-smudged vinyl smock she'd worn for the morning art project and hung it on a hook in the closet, then headed through the activity room and out to the playground to open the gate, which was kept locked at all times. To keep not only the children in, but strangers out. With a man as powerful and influential as the senator, and the day-care center on the grounds of his estate, one could never be too careful.

Her father stood on the other side, dressed for golf and wearing his plastic politician's smile. Then her eyes settled on the man standing beside him.

Whoa.

When Margaret said British diplomat, Rowena had pictured a stuffy, balding, forty-something elitist with an ego to match his bulging Swiss bank accounts. This man was her age or close to it, and there was nothing stuffy about him. His hair was the color of dried wheat, closely cropped and stylishly spiky. His eyes were a piercing, almost eerie shade of blue that *had* to be tinted contacts, and were curtained with thick dark lashes that any woman would sell her soul for. And though he might have been a royal in title, the shadow of neatly trimmed blond stubble and a small scar bisecting his left brow gave him an edgy look. He was several inches taller than the senator, which put him somewhere around six-three. As lean as he was, he should have looked lanky; instead, he was perfectly proportioned.

The rebel in her said, *Come to mama.* But the logical Rowena, the mature adult, knew from experience that powerful, sinfully attractive men were the worst kind of trouble. And unfortunately, the best kind of fun. Until they took what they wanted and moved on to greener pastures. Or, as had happened with her son, Dylan's, father, knocked her up and abandoned her. She punched in her code, opened the gate and let them in.

"Sweetheart, I'd like you to meet Colin Middlebury," the senator said—*sweetheart* being a term he only used when he was milking his family-man image. "Colin, this is my daughter, Rowena."

The man leveled those remarkable eyes on her and flashed her a grin that was as much smirk as smile, and her heart went pitter-patter.

"Miss Tate," he said in a silky smooth voice punctuated by a crisp accent that, if she were still the type to swoon, would have had her fanning her face. "It's a pleasure to meet you."

Oh, the pleasure is all mine, believe me. She glanced over at her father, who was wearing his *behave or else* look.

"Mr. Middlebury, welcome to L.A.," she said.

"Please, call me Colin." His grin, the slight lift of his left brow, made it feel more like a dare. And when he shook her hand, she felt a delightful little tingle.

Wow, it had been a really long time since a man had made her tingle. Most of the men her father brought around were stodgy old politicians with clammy hands, roaming eyes and greedy smiles. The kind whose power in politics made them believe they were irresistible to anything with two legs and a pair of breasts.

"Colin will be staying here at the mansion while we iron out the details of a treaty I'm sponsoring," her father said. "Two or three weeks."

This was usually the worst part of being a politician's daughter—having to play the role of the polite hostess, when on the inside she was grinding her teeth. But when the guest looked like Colin Middlebury? Well, he could be the world's biggest jerk, but at least the view was nice.

Looking in the direction of the playground, her father asked, "Where is my grandson?"

"He's upstairs with his speech therapist," she said. The main floor of the building served as the day-care center, while the upper floor was set up to accommodate a variety of physical, speech and occupational therapy equipment. That way her son, Dylan, could receive all the therapy he needed and she could run the day care without interruption. Her father's idea, of course. Only the best for his grandson.

"When will he be finished? I'd like Colin to meet him."

She glanced at her watch. "Not for another thirty minutes. And he shouldn't be disturbed."

"Another time," Colin said, and asked Rowena, "Will you be joining us at Estavez for dinner tonight?"

Heck yes. She would love to. But a stern look from her father made the correct answer to that question more than obvious.

"Maybe some other time," she told Colin.

"Colin," her father said, "why don't you and I take a quick tour inside."

"Fantastic," Colin said, and maybe it was just the accent, but he sounded genuinely excited.

"I started this project two years ago," the senator told him proudly as they walked to the building, not mentioning—he never did—that the initial idea had been hers.

"Hey, Row!"

Rowena looked across the playground to where Patricia Adams, the assistant manager—and also her best friend— stood watching the kids on the monkey bars. She fanned her face and mouthed the word *wow*.

No kidding.

Only a few minutes passed before her father and Colin reemerged from the building, and she could see instantly that the senator was in a huff about something.

"It would seem that someone left paint on the edge of one of the tables and it's gotten onto Colin's pants," he told her, and while his tone was reasonable, his jaw was clenched and his eyes had that if-I-get-any-angrier-I'm-going-to-pop look about them.

Colin, in contrast, seemed unfazed, despite a rather large magenta smudge on his left pant leg. "It's really no problem," he said.

"It's a water-based, washable paint," Rowena told him. "A little soap and water should take that right out. I'm sure Betty, our housekeeper, can take care of it for you. But if for whatever reason they're ruined, I'll replace them."

"That certainly won't be necessary," Colin said.

"Well, we should let you get back to work," her father said, flashing his plastic smile. "Colin, would you excuse me and my daughter for a moment? I just need a quick word with her."

Oh boy, here we go.

"Of course. I'll start back up to the house."

She followed her father into the building, then, he turned to her and said, "Rowena, all I ask when I bring a guest in is that you have the center clean and presentable. Was it too much trouble to wipe up a paint spill? Colin is *royalty,* for God's sake, an *earl,* not to mention a war hero. What possible reason could you have to be so rude?"

If he was a war hero, he'd probably had a lot worse than paint spill on his pants, she thought, but she didn't dare say it.

Like so many times before, she swallowed her pride—and even managed not to gag at the bitter aftertaste—

saying, "I'm sorry, we must have missed some when we cleaned up. I'll be more careful next time."

"If there is a next time. If you can't manage something as simple as wiping up paint, how can you be expected to adequately care for children?"

"I'm sorry," she said. She didn't know what else to say.

"After all I've done for you and Dylan..." He shook his head, as if he had no words to describe her audacity and selfishness. Then for dramatic effect, he stormed out in a huff.

She slumped against the wall, angry and frustrated and yes, *hurt*. But not defeated. He could keep knocking her down, but she would always get back up again.

"Hey, Row?"

Tricia stood in the doorway, looking concerned. "You okay?"

She took a deep breath, squared her shoulders and forced what probably looked more like a grimace than a smile. "No big deal."

"I heard what he said about the paint. That was my fault. I asked April to wipe the tables down and I guess I forget to check if she'd missed anything. I know how picky he is when he brings people in. I should have been more careful. I'm so sorry."

"Tricia, if it hadn't been the paint, it would have been something else. You know that he *always* finds something."

"It's not right the way he treats you."

"I put him through a lot."

"You've changed, Row. You've pulled your life together."

"But I wouldn't have been able to do it without his help. You can't deny that he's done a lot for me and Dylan."

"That's what he wants you to think. But that doesn't

make it okay for him to treat you like an indentured servant. You would manage just fine on your own."

She wanted to believe that, but the last time she'd been on her own she had made a total mess of her life.

"You know the offer still stands. If you and Dylan want to come stay with me for a while..."

And the instant she left, he would cut off not just her but Dylan, as well. And without the money to pay for his medical care, her father would have all the ammunition he needed to take Dylan away from her. She'd been hearing that threat since the day Dylan was born. It was the ultimate punishment, and she didn't doubt for a second that he would do it.

"I can't, Tricia, but I love you for offering."

Her own irresponsibility and carelessness were what had gotten her into this mess, and she was the only one who could get herself out.

Colin had never put much stock in rumors. In a royal family, even on the outermost fringes, gossip spread like a disease. Which was why, when he heard the speculation about the senator's daughter, out of fairness and respect, he reserved judgment. And maybe he was missing something, but she'd seemed all right to him. Of course, she could have had two heads and hooves for feet and he would have been perfectly gracious.

This assignment was Colin's first go as a diplomat, and certainly not somewhere he had intended to be at this point in his life—or ever, for that matter—but he was making the best of an unfortunate situation. He had been warned that when dealing with American politicians, especially one as powerful and influential as Senator Tate, he would be wise to watch his back. The senator was a man who got things done. When he put the weight of his office behind legislation, his colleagues naturally fell in line. The royal family was counting on Colin to ensure that the tech treaty, a crucial piece of legislation for both the U.K. and the U.S., became law.

Too many high-profile instances of phone and internet hacking had been occurring in both the U.K. and the U.S. A tech treaty would give international law enforcement the tools to see that the guilty parties were brought to justice.

Due to illegal hacking, President Morrow had been outed as having an illegitimate daughter by the press at his own inaugural ball in front of family, friends and celebrities. Even worse, his supposed illegitimate daughter, Ariella Winthrop, had been standing a few feet away from him when the news broke and was taken by complete surprise herself.

The U.S. was finally willing to negotiate. It was up to Colin to see it through.

He'd made it nearly halfway up the bricked trail to the mansion when Senator Tate caught up to him, saying, "Again, my apologies."

"As I said, it's not a problem."

"It's no secret that Rowena had problems in the past," the senator said. "She has worked hard to overcome them."

Still, the senator seemed to keep her on a very short leash. It was silly to get so upset over something as simple as spilled paint.

"I think we've all done things we're not proud of."

The senator was quiet for several seconds, then, looking troubled, said, "Can I be direct with you, Colin?"

"Of course."

"I understand that you have something of a reputation as a womanizer."

"I do?"

"I don't mean to imply that I would hold that against

you," the senator said. "How you lead your life is your business."

Colin wouldn't deny that he had dated his share of women, but he was no cad. He never dated a woman without first making it absolutely clear that he was in no hurry to settle down, and he never promised exclusivity.

"Sir, this so-called reputation of mine sounds a bit hyperbolic."

"You're young, in your prime, and I don't fault you for playing the field."

Colin sensed an unspoken "however" at the end of that sentence.

"Under normal circumstances I wouldn't even bring it up, but I've welcomed you into my home for an extended stay, and I should make it clear that there are certain ground rules I expect you to follow."

Ground rules?

"My daughter can be very…impulsive and in the past has been a target for unscrupulous men who think they can use her to get to me. Or simply just use her."

"Sir, let me assure you—"

He held up a hand to stop him. "It's not an accusation."

It certainly felt like one.

"That said, I must insist that as long as you're staying in my home, you are to consider my daughter off-limits."

Well, it didn't get much more direct than that.

"Can I count on you to do the right thing, son?"

"Of course," Colin said, unsure if he should feel slighted or amused or if he should pity the senator. "I'm here to work on the treaty."

"Well, then," the senator said, "Let's get to work."

Two

After a long day of collaboration with the senator that was encouragingly productive, and dinner out with him and several of his friends, Colin found a quiet, dark corner by the pool to relax. It was blessedly out of view of the mansion, and the only place that he felt truly alone on the estate. And he needed his alone time. He stretched out in a lounge chair and gazed up at a clear, star-filled sky while he sipped a glass of the senator's finest scotch.

When his phone rang he was surprised to see his sister's number flash across the screen. It was only 5:30 a.m. in London.

"You're up early," he said in lieu of a hello.

"Mother's having a rough night," she told him, "so I was up watching television. I just wanted to check in and see how you're enjoying your stay there."

"It's been…interesting."

He told her about the senator's warning, and at first she was convinced he was joking.

"It's the God's honest truth," he assured her.

"Her father actually told you that she's *off-limits?*"

"In those exact words."

"How unbelievably rude and tactless!"

"Apparently I have a *reputation* with the *ladies.*"

With Rowena's flame-red hair and striking, emerald-green bedroom eyes, he couldn't deny that under different circumstances he would have been interested. *Very* interested. But he was more than capable of resisting a beautiful woman.

"Maybe you should come home," Matty said.

She meant to London, of course, and though he'd spent most of his recovery there, it hadn't felt like home any more than it had when he was a child. Home to him was boarding school, then later whichever country he'd been stationed in.

"You've been through so much, and you're still healing," Matilda insisted. Twenty years his senior, she had always been more of a parent than a sibling. But more so after the helicopter crash. Yes, he was lucky to be alive, but dwelling on the past was counterproductive. The worst of his wounds had healed and he needed to get on with his life. Not that he could ever expect to forget completely, nor would he want to. He was proud of his service and honored to defend his country. Deep down he would always be a warrior.

"I know you're doing this for the family's sake," Matilda said, "but, Colin, *politics?* It's so…*beneath* you."

Having spent most of her life distanced from the royal family and isolated from the real world, Matilda couldn't truly grasp the need for the treaty. "I need to do this. The family's privacy has been violated countless times, our reputation damaged. This has to stop. We need the treaty."

"I'm just worried about you," she said. "Are you staying warm?"

He laughed. "I'm in Southern California, Matty. It doesn't get cold here." Unlike Washington, where he'd made a brief stop before flying to the West Coast. There the bitter wind and subzero temperatures seeped into his bones, reminding him, with aches and twinges, that he had a while to go before he was fully recovered.

They chatted for a few more minutes, and Matilda started to yawn.

"You should try to get some more sleep," he told her.

"Promise you'll take care of yourself."

"I promise. Love you, Matty, and give my best to Mother."

"Love you, too."

He disconnected, slid his phone back into his pants pocket and closed his eyes, going over in his head all that they had covered this afternoon, and how much more work they had ahead of them. Thorough as the senator was, he insisted they pick the treaty apart, section by section, line by line. It would be a slow and agonizing process. And it would be given the same scrutiny in the U.K. before anything was set in stone.

At some point he must have drifted off, because he was startled awake by a loud splash. He jerked up in the chair, blinking furiously, briefly disoriented by his surroundings. He'd lived so many places that at times they all blurred together, and when he woke from a deep sleep it took him a moment to get his bearings.

Senator's mansion. Pool deck. *Got it.*

Had he actually heard a splash, or had it just been a dream? He noticed movement in the water at the far end of the pool. Backlit by the glow emanating from under the surface, the blurry outline of a figure cut though the water. Then, as the swimmer came up for air, he saw the unmistakable flash of flaming red hair.

Rowena dove back under, then resurfaced when she reached the opposite side, not ten feet from where he sat. She flipped over, arms slicing through the water as she pushed off the side. He sat there, transfixed, hypnotized by the graceful glide of her body, the practiced, even strokes that took her to the opposite end of the pool, then back again. It went on like that for a while, until she finally stopped at the end farthest from him and hung on to the edge, seemingly exhausted and out of breath. But she couldn't have rested more than a minute before she started the process all over again.

After a few more laps he began to think about the senator, his ridiculous *ground rules,* and how Colin's sitting there watching his daughter might be misconstrued. And the more he thought about it, the more it seemed inappropriate. He could sneak away, but if someone were to see him that would definitely make it seem as if he had something to hide. By not leaving the second she dove into the pool, without even realizing it, he had created something of a dilemma for himself. At this point, it seemed that the wise thing to do would be to politely announce his presence, then get the hell out.

Still fuming over the berating she'd received from her father in front of her staff today when he learned that she'd gone thirty dollars over budget on art supplies for the month, Rowena pushed herself harder than usual, working out her frustration, swimming until her arms and legs felt rubbery and her shoulders ached.

Three years, two months and six days sober, and the senator was still waiting for her to fail.

And while she wasn't denying she'd made a lot of mistakes, they were mistakes that she had since owned up to, and paid her penance for a million times over.

She had done everything her father had asked of her, but it still wasn't enough. Maybe it would never be enough for him. She would always be the bad seed, always chasing after his love, trying to please him, but never quite making the cut.

It was tough to impress a man who didn't want to be impressed.

By the time she was finished swimming she was so exhausted she barely had the strength to hoist herself up over the side and out of the water.

"That was quite a workout," an unfamiliar and sinister-sounding voice said from somewhere behind her in the dark.

Startled, she whipped around, seeing only the shadow of a very large and intimidating figure. Her heart stopped, then picked up triple time, alarm flooding her veins with adrenaline, her automatic first thought being rapist or serial killer. In that split second she imagined José the pool boy finding her bloated, discolored corpse floating in the water the following morning, or some unfortunate jogger finding her in the woods along the jogging path in one of the city parks.

Her brain said *run,* and she took an instinctive step back—right off the edge of the pool. She felt herself falling backward, thought, *Okay, now what?* and then a hand shot out of the darkness and locked firmly around her wrist, tugging her upright, to her imminent doom.

She jerked her arm back, expecting him to let go. Instead she managed to knock both herself and her would-be attacker off balance and sent them both careening into the pool.

They landed with a splash, the voice she'd heard suddenly replaying like a tape recorder in her head, only this time it sounded vaguely familiar. This time she heard the crisp accent, the smooth-as-caramel tone that really wasn't sinister after all. And as he surfaced beside her, sputtering and cursing, all she could think was that her father was going to *kill* her.

If Colin didn't get to her first.

"Why in the *bloody hell* did you do that?" he said, treading water.

"I'm so sorry," she said.

He grabbed the edge of the pool and hoisted himself up. But the fact that she wasn't about to be murdered left her so weak with relief that when she tried to pull herself up onto the deck, her arms crumpled and she slid back into the water instead.

"Allow me," he said, reaching down to help her. When she hesitated, he said in an exasperated voice, "Just take my hand, for God's sake."

It was either accept his help or swim to the steps at the opposite end, and she honestly wasn't sure she had the strength.

She grabbed his outstretched hand and with hardly any effort at all he hauled her out of the water. He was strong, which had her questioning how she'd managed to get him into the water in the first place. Maybe the adrenaline had given her superhuman strength. Now she felt weak and trembly and cold.

Colin grabbed her towel from the chair where she'd left it, but instead of using it on himself, he wrapped it around her shoulders. Her modest one-piece could hardly be considered revealing, yet she couldn't help feeling exposed.

His soggy slacks and sweater were a pretty good indication that he hadn't been out there to swim. Unless he'd been planning to skinny-dip.

She wouldn't have minded seeing that.

He pulled an expensive-looking cell phone from the pocket of his soggy slacks. She cringed as he gave it a shake, jabbed the home button a few times and got nothing.

If he told her father about this, she was dead meat.

"I am so sorry. I didn't know anyone else was out here. I usually have the pool all to myself."

"I didn't mean to startle you," he said, ringing water from the sleeves of his sweater. "I was sitting by the pool and I must have dozed off. I woke up when you dove in."

"Your phone—can it be salvaged?"

"I doubt it," he said, and shoved it back into his pocket.

His sweater wasn't looking too promising, either. Her father was going to have a field day with this one. "I am so sorry, Colin. First your pants, now this."

He gave up on the sweater, which had gone all saggy and misshapen, and said, "Could you spare me a towel?"

"Of course!" Where were her manners? It was the least she could do, since, in the process of trying not to get herself murdered, she had murdered his phone instead and, from the looks of it, his sweater…and were those *leather* shoes?

"They're in the pool house."

He followed her, his soles squeaking against the ceramic tile. She prayed he wasn't wearing an expensive and nonwaterproof wristwatch.

The door was locked, and she didn't have her keys, so she dug behind the loose strip of siding beside the door frame and pulled out the spare. Once inside, she switched on the lights, blinking against the sudden brightness.

While it was technically a pool house, it was the size, and had all the amenities, of a studio apartment.

Colin kicked off his shoes and followed her inside. She stepped into the bathroom, which had its own door leading to the pool area, and grabbed a beach towel from the shelf. She walked back out just as Colin was peeling the wet sweater over his head, uncovering a chest and midriff that were a testament to years of dedication to fitness, and an abdomen hard with rippling muscles. Slim hips and lean, strong arms gave proportion to what, under the clingy fabric of his slacks, were clearly long and muscular legs. Then he turned to toss the ruined garment out the door, and she sucked in a quiet breath.

Patchy, pink burn scars that were fully healed, yet somehow still looked painfully fresh, started just below his shoulders and ran down the entire width of his back, disappearing beneath the waist of his pants.

She wiped the surprise from her face as he turned back around. Aside from the scars, his body couldn't have been more perfect.

He held out his hand and said, "Towel?"

She handed it to him. "I'm sorry."

"You're forgiven," he said, sounding exasperated. "Now would you *please* stop apologizing."

"Sorr—"

He shot her a look.

She shrugged. "Habit."

Watching him dry his magnificently toned pecs and thick arms, she felt a shimmery *za-zing* of awareness, in places that hadn't *za-zing*ed in a *long* time. Which was the absolute *last* thing she should be thinking about right now.

He seemed like a pretty reasonable guy. She went out on a limb and asked, "Is there any way that we could maybe not tell my father about this?"

He flashed her one of those adorable grins. "It'll be our little secret."

The idea of having a secret with him, big or little, made

her heart skip. Here she was, twenty-six and reacting like a schoolgirl with a crush.

"The senator, he demands perfection?" Colin asked.

That was something of an understatement. "He does have very high standards."

"For what it's worth, I was impressed. With the day care, I mean."

"Thanks." And for some stupid reason, she heard herself saying, "It was my idea."

Rather than a brush-off, or a *sure it was* look, he appeared genuinely interested. "Was it?"

She should quit while she was ahead, but she couldn't seem to make her mouth stop moving. "My father has always run on an all-American family-man platform." Ironic, considering what a negligent father he actually was. Work always came first. "Among other things one of his causes has been affordable day care for working families. His own staff was no exception. So opening a day care for them seemed like a logical solution. It would be good for his career, and for the people who work for him. And it has been."

"So it's as much your project as his?"

Uh oh. She shook her head, laughed nervously. "*No,* no, not at all, it's definitely his project. Although I did have fun helping with the plans, then watching it all come together. I toured day-care centers all over the city and scoured the internet for ideas."

Looking puzzled, he said, "So how then is it not your project?"

She really needed to stop talking. "It's not my name on the checks."

"Writing the checks is the easy part," he said, as though he knew that from experience. "It sounds as if you did the hard part. All the *real* work."

If it got back to the senator that she was taking credit for the day care, he would come unhinged.

"My part of it was nothing, really."

"For *nothing,* you seem quite proud of what you've done. And it sounds as if you should be."

But it wasn't worth the hassle if it meant stepping on her father's very large toes. Why had she even brought this up in the first place?

"You look nervous," he said.

"Sometimes my mouth works independently from my brain, and I say things I shouldn't."

"Would it help to say that what you and I discuss in private will never reach the senator's ears?"

She blew out a relieved breath. "I would really appreciate that."

"Though it's a shame you feel the need to hide your accomplishments."

It was a survival instinct. "My father and I, our relationship is…complicated. It's easier for everyone if I don't rock the boat."

"I think I understand."

Did he? Really?

She looked at the clock. "Wow, I didn't realize how late it is. I really have to get inside or Betty is going to think I drowned."

"Betty, the housekeeper?"

She nodded. "She sits with Dylan while I do my laps. I'm usually only gone forty minutes…." She paused, working the time out in her head. "Did you say that you woke up when I dove into the water?"

"The splash roused me."

Yet he didn't say anything to her until *after* she swam her laps. So what was he doing all that time?

"Yes," he said, as if he were reading her mind. "I was

watching you swim, which I know was a violation of your privacy. My only excuse, flimsy as it is, is that I was mesmerized." He reached for her hand, drawing it between his, and...*talk about tingles.* His hands were big and strong and a little rough. "I hope you'll accept my apology."

Damn, this guy was *good.* She made the mistake of looking up into his eyes, and felt herself being sucked into their unearthly blue depths. A woman could drown in eyes like that.

His eyes never leaving hers, he said, "Why is it that when something is forbidden, it makes you want it that much more?"

Come and get me, she wanted to say. Then she reminded herself that he was a politician, and no matter how sincere he may have looked or sounded, he possessed the ability to lie through his royal teeth. And very convincingly.

But a little innocent flirting never hurt anyone. Right?

His eyes searched hers, then dipped lower, settling on her mouth, which of course made her look at *his* mouth, and all she could think was how kissable his lips looked, and how much she wanted to be the one kissing them.

He lifted her hand to his lips, brushing a kiss across the back, and the earth pitched under her feet. It had been a long time since a man's lips had touched *any* part of her body.

"It was a pleasure talking with you," he said.

Yes it was. "Maybe we could do it again."

"Maybe," he said, letting go of her hand. But he did it slowly, his fingers sliding across hers, pausing as they reached the very tips.

Don't go, she thought. Only because she didn't have the guts to say it out loud. But apparently he wasn't a mind reader after all, because he turned, grabbed his shoes and sweater and walked away.

She watched in silence as he disappeared into the dark, wishing they really could do it again, but knowing that it was better if they didn't. Not that it hadn't been fun flirting with him. But it could never be more than that.

When Rowena got to her suite, Betty, their live-in maid, was stretched out on the sofa watching *Dynasty* reruns on cable.

"That must have been some swim," she said, sitting up and switching off the television, her tight gray curls pressed flat against the back of her head.

"Betty, I'm so sorry. I didn't mean to take so long."

"As if I have somewhere more exciting to be," Betty said. She didn't ask Rowena what had taken so long, and Rowena didn't indulge.

Betty slowly rose from the couch, stretching her arthritic back. She had been with the family since Rowena was a baby. She taught Rowena to bake cookies, told her about the birds and the bees and took her for her first bra, since her mother couldn't be bothered. And when Rowena was battling her addictions, Betty was the only person who never lost faith in her. But she was getting older, slowing down physically, and eventually it would be time for her to retire.

"Did Dylan wake up?"

"He didn't make a peep."

"Thanks for watching him," she said, giving Betty a hug.

"No problem, sweetie. Tomorrow night, same time?"

"If you don't mind."

As she walked her to the door, Rowena casually asked, "So, what do you think of my father's guest?"

"Mr. Middlebury? He seems friendly and very polite. A

bit of a flirt, I suppose, and boy is he a hottie." She looked back at Rowena. "Do they still call attractive men hotties?"

"Hottie works."

"Well, then, he definitely is one. Maybe, if I were thirty years younger..." she said with a grin. "Why do you ask?"

Rowena shrugged. "Just curious."

"Are you interested?"

She shook her head. "Not at all. You know I don't date politicians."

"Oh, he's not a politician. He's just here as a favor to his family. They seemed to think that because he's a war hero, he would have more of an influence in Washington."

Not a politician? *Interesting.*

"You seem to know an awful lot about him," Rowena said.

"We've chatted a time or two. You should talk to him."

She didn't mention that she already had. "I'll think about it."

After Betty left, Rowena checked on Dylan, who was sound asleep in his crib, and then she showered, changed into her pajamas and crawled into bed with her computer to check her email, which, as usual, was mostly junk.

She was about to close her laptop, but on a whim, opened her browser instead and typed in Colin's name.

A page of results popped up on the screen, but instead of social columns about a womanizing earl and his exploits, what she found was news stories about Colin Middlebury the war hero.

An honor he had clearly earned.

During his last tour in the Middle East, a helicopter he was a passenger in crashed. He was thrown from the craft and, with a shattered leg, had crawled back, dragging the pilot, who had been knocked unconscious, away from the wreckage. But before they could reach a safe distance the helicopter burst into flames. Both men suffered severe burns, and Colin spent first a month in the hospital, then another eight weeks in a rehab center.

It sounded as if Colin had been incredibly lucky. Other than the small scar bisecting his brow, he had no obvious marks. Until he took off his clothes, that is. And the last thing she needed to be doing was thinking about Colin with his clothes off. Did she miss dating? Sometimes. But there was nothing Rowena needed that she couldn't provide herself. In or out of the bedroom.

That didn't mean it wouldn't be fun.

Three

The following day seemed to drag by, as if time were moving through a vat of molasses. Rowena tried to keep busy, ordering supplies, working on lesson plans and scouring the internet for craft ideas. Then right in the middle of a task, a vision of Colin, standing in the pool house, his chest bare, his arms thick with sinew, would pop into her head and she'd completely forget what she was doing.

Would he be at the pool again tonight, or when he said maybe, had he just been humoring her? Did he really mean *no way lady?* Maybe after they talked, he didn't find her quite so attractive after all.

She felt nervous and distracted all afternoon, and during dinner, while Dylan chattered away about his day, she was only half listening. What if Colin really did show? What then?

Even if he liked her, and she liked him, he was only here for a few weeks. It's not as if they could ever have any kind of relationship.

She was a responsible adult. Someone's *mother*. Her days of brief affairs and one-night stands had ended the day she found out she was pregnant. It was too…undignified.

It shouldn't have mattered if Colin was at the pool or not. So why, when she went to take her swim and she found the chairs empty, was she so disappointed?

When she was done, as she was walking back to her suite, she thought about taking a quick detour to Colin's suite. Only to tell him again that she had enjoyed their talk, and to let him know that if he needed anything, all he had to do was ask.

Rowena, she imagined him saying, *all I need is you.*

He would be shirtless, of course, and possibly just out of the shower, with droplets of water dotting his pecs. His hair would be wet and spiky. He would hold out his hand, and though she would hesitate for several seconds, she would take it. He would pull her into his room, closing the door behind them….

At that point she made herself keep walking until she reached her own suite. As unlikely as it was that would ever really happen, it scared her to think what would happen if it did.

The following morning she managed not to think about him much at all, until she was walking up to the mansion and saw Colin and her father's attorney sitting on the back patio.

"Hello, Colin," she said with a smile, her heart lifting at the sight of him, only to flop back down and land with a sickening thud when he replied, "Hello, Miss Tate."

He didn't even crack a smile.

'Nuff said. She squared her shoulders and kept walking. She had no reason to be upset or feel slighted. They'd talked *one* time. It wasn't as if he'd promised they would

see each other again. To avoid seeing him again she left through the front door, taking a different route back, walking all the way down the driveway to the road, then up a quarter mile to the day-care center.

"Why did you go the long way?" Tricia asked.

"Good exercise," Rowena told her, then hid in her office for the rest of the morning, refusing to feel sorry for herself. She was being silly, that's all. All the time she spent cooped up on the estate must be taking its toll.

In the afternoon a feisty ten-year-old named Davis, whose mother worked for the senator soliciting donations, took a tumble off the monkey bars and Rowena sat with him, holding an ice pack on his bruised and swollen arm, until his mother arrived and rushed him off to the E.R. for X-rays.

She filled out an accident report and all the other appropriate documentation, then sat through a berating from her father—in front of Dylan, no less—because naturally it was her fault.

"Dabis godda owie taday," Dylan said as she tucked him into bed that night.

She pulled the covers up to his chin. "Yes, Davis got an owie. But his mommy called and said it was just a *small* owie. Nothing broken."

There was genuine relief in his big hazel eyes. Having been through so much himself, Dylan was exceptionally empathetic for a boy his age. And though he might have physically disabilities, he was smart as a whip and wise beyond his very short two and a half years.

"Papa mad at you," he said.

"No, baby, he's not mad," she lied. "He was just worried about Davis. But Davis is fine, so everything is okay." She got so tired of making excuses for her father's behavior. Dylan adored him. He was the only grandparent Dylan had, but Dylan was exceptionally smart. It wouldn't be long before he began to understand the kind of man his grandfather really was.

As she leaned down and kissed him good-night, Dylan asked the same question he had every night since he'd learned to talk.

"I gedda big bed?"

She sighed and tousled his curly red mop of hair. "Yes, sweetie, you'll get a big-boy bed very soon."

She felt guilty for depriving him of something he wanted so badly, but she just wasn't ready to take the chance. In his crib she knew he was safe. In a regular bed, if he had a seizure or even just rolled too far to one side, he could fall out and hurt himself.

Accepting her empty promise with a hopeful smile, the way he always did, and with his favorite toy race car clutched in his hand, he rolled onto his side and closed his eyes. He was so tiny for his age. So small and defenseless. She wasn't ready for him to grow up.

She leaned down, kissed him one last time and whispered, "I love you."

"Wuboo, too," he said sleepily.

She switched off his light, checked that the baby monitor was on, then slipped out of the room. As much as she needed a break by the end of the day, and a little time to herself, she hated leaving him alone. Until a year ago she'd kept him in bed with her, until the pediatrician warned that coddling him might only inhibit his progress. But it was so hard to let go, to relinquish control.

Rowena changed into her swimsuit, but she still had twenty minutes before Betty would be there to babysit, so she switched on the television. It was tuned to the American News Service—the cable network that had broken the presidential paternity scandal—and the anchor, Angelica

Pierce, was reporting, as was often the case lately, on recent developments in the story. And Angelica seemed to take a sick sort of satisfaction in relaying the details.

Having been the target of rumors and speculation a time or two herself, Rowena could relate. Although in her case, the rumors usually were true. But she was never outed in front of hundreds of people.

Angelica Pierce was saying something about paternity and blood tests, and how both Ariella, the president's alleged illegitimate daughter, and Eleanor, his high school sweetheart, were unavailable for comment. The devilish gleam in Angelica's eyes said she was out for blood and thoroughly enjoying the scandal.

Rowena was about to switch the channel when she was struck by a sense of familiarity so intense it actually gave her goose bumps. Something about Angelica had always annoyed Rowena, but she had always attributed it to ANS's sleazy reporting. She'd also thought that the woman looked vaguely familiar, and suddenly she realized why.

She reached for the phone and dialed her boarding school buddy Caroline Crenshaw. Until recently a public relations expert at the White House, Cara kept Rowena up to date on all the juicy D.C. gossip—confirming time after time that Rowena had made the right decision leaving Washington permanently. Only when Max, Cara's fiancé, answered did Rowena remember the time difference and realize that it was nearly eleven-thirty there. "Sorry to be calling so late," she said. "Is Cara still awake?"

"She's right here," Max said. There was a brief pause, and then Cara's voice came on the line. Sounding worried, she asked, "Hey, Row, is everything okay?"

After receiving countless, random drunken midnight phone calls from Rowena, of course Cara would think the worst. "Everything is fine. I had a quick question for you and I completely forgot about the time difference."

"That's a relief. I thought maybe something had happened to Dylan."

Or did she think that Rowena had backslidden and gotten herself in trouble again? And could Rowena blame her if she had? "Dylan is tucked away safe and sound in bed. Do you by any chance have the television on?"

"Actually, we do. We're in bed watching the news."

"NCN?"

"Of course."

She'd assumed as much, since Max had made a name for himself as a hotshot political anchor and talk show host at National Cable News. "Can you switch on ANS for a minute?"

"Sure, why?"

"You've seen Angelica Pierce?"

"Sure. I've actually met her a couple of times. Now there's a woman who knows what she wants and will do anything to get it. I pity the person who tries to stand in her way."

"Does she look like anyone else to you?"

"I don't know. There's always been something about her that bugs me, but I think that has a lot to do with her working for ANS and their sleazy smear campaign against the president."

"Take a really good look at her, and think back to boarding school."

"Boarding school?"

"Think Madeline Burch."

"Oh, my gosh, I forgot all about her. What a loon!"

Madeline had been an unstable, mousy plain Jane who insisted that she had a secret wealthy father and that her mother had been paid big hush-hush money not to talk about him. Which only led the students to believe that she was nuttier than a fruitcake, a label that seemed to push Madeline even further over the edge, until her behavior became so erratic and unpredictable she was eventually expelled. "So, look at Angelica, and think of Madeline."

"Wow, you're right. She does sort of look like her, but a hell of a lot prettier and more glamorous."

"Do you think it could be her?"

"She would have had to change her looks and her name. Why would she do that?"

"That's the real question, I guess. News anchors are supposed to be objective, but she takes an awful lot of satisfaction in smearing President Morrow. You know she wants to take him down."

"Maybe she's just a bitch," Cara suggested.

"And if she is Madeline Burch?"

"I'm still not sure why she would go through all that trouble, but it couldn't hurt to look into it. I'll see what I can dig up from my old contacts."

"I'll try the internet."

"Give me a couple of days and I'll get back to you."

After they hung up, Rowena logged on to Google to see what she could find about Madeline, but there was virtually no information about her after the incident at Woodlawn Academy, when she had attacked a student who called her a liar and a freak. When Rowena did a similar search on Angelica Pierce, the woman didn't seem to exist before her college days.

When Betty knocked on the door at nine, Rowena still hadn't found anything useful.

She shot a quick email to Cara explaining what she had—or more specifically *hadn't*—found, then headed down to the pool. She was so wrapped up in her own thoughts, she almost didn't notice the faint outline of some-

one sitting in a chaise—Colin's chaise. It was unlikely that
anyone but him would be out there, and even more unlikely
that someone else would pick that exact same chair to sit
in. And despite his chilly greeting that morning, it would
be rude not to go over and say hello.

As she drew closer, she could see that his head had
lolled slightly to one side and his eyes were closed, his
breathing slow and deep. Cupped in his hands and resting in his lap was a large mug of what looked like brewed
tea. Not the smartest place to hold a hot drink. Suppose
when she dove in, the splash startled him and it spilled?
He could do some serious damage.

"Colin?" she said softly so she wouldn't alarm him, but
he didn't budge. He looked so peaceful. Maybe she didn't
have to wake him; maybe if she just took the cup and set
it on the table…

She reached down, never imagining that she would
have her hands quite this close to his crotch tonight. Or
any night.

Very gently, using the tips of her fingers, she clutched
the cup by the rim and began to gingerly lift it from his
lap. She'd lifted about six inches when she glanced up to
his face. His eyes were open and looking at her.

As cold tea soaked his trousers, Colin belatedly realized that until Rowena had gotten the cup a safe distance
from his crotch, he should have kept his eyes closed. But
when a man dreamed he was with a woman, then opened
his eyes to find her hand an inch from his fly, it was tough
not to watch the action. And for several tense seconds, it
wasn't the cup he thought she was reaching for.

"Oh, my God. I am so sorry," Rowena said, looking as
though she wasn't sure if she should laugh or cry. "I can't
believe I just did that. Please tell me that wasn't hot."

He set the cup on the ground beside him. "It was rather cold, actually."

She winced, "I didn't...*damage* anything down there, did I?"

He'd managed to catch the cup just in time. "Everything *down there* is fine."

She handed him her towel. "I don't know how much help this will be."

He pushed himself out of the chair, leaning over to inspect the front of his pants, then handed the towel back. "I think it's pretty hopeless at this point."

"For the record, I was moving it because I thought it might spill. And yes, I get the irony."

What tea hadn't soaked into the linen went straight through to his Skivvies. "The staff is going to think I'm off my rocker. Walking in one night in dripping-wet clothes, the next looking as if I soiled myself."

She bit her lip, probably to keep from laughing, then said, "I could run up to your room and get you clean pants. Or you could borrow some swim trunks. There are always extras in the pool house. There's bound to be something that fits."

The last thing he needed was her father possibly seeing her walking in or out of his suite. At least here, by the pool, no one could see them. Not without leaving the mansion, which no one seemed to do after dark. "Swim trunks will be fine."

"Let's go look."

She rushed to the pool house, opened the door and switched on the lights. In the dark it had looked as if she was wearing a dress. Now he realized it was a cover-up, and underneath she wore...*well, hello there, bikini.* He wondered if she had worn that purposely, in case he happened to be at the pool again. Didn't matter either way. She was off-limits.

"There's a shelf in the bathroom with extra suits," she told him. "Take whatever you need."

Colin found a pair of trunks close to his size and pulled them off the shelf. He peeled off his wet slacks and boxer briefs, noticing, as the cold wet fabric touched the top of his legs, that the tails of his shirt hadn't been spared, either. He took that off, too, and pulled the suit on. When he stepped out of the bathroom, Rowena was standing in the kitchen, bent over, looking in the refrigerator with her back to him. The cover-up was hiked up to reveal the very smooth curve of her behind and the backs of her creamy thighs.

Bloody hell.

"Found a pair," he said.

She straightened and turned, a can of soda in her hand. She looked briefly at the trunks, then her eyes drifted upward.

Knowing what she was thinking, he said, "My shirt was wet, too."

"They're big," she said. "The trunks, I mean."

"Well, it was these or a Speedo."

She opened her mouth to say something, then shook her head as if she'd decided that whatever it was was probably best left unsaid. "Want to split a soda, or would you like something stronger?"

What he wanted, he couldn't have. What he needed was a cold shower. And what he had to do was leave.

And he would leave, just as soon as he finished his drink. "Soda is fine."

She pulled two glasses from the cupboard, poured the soda, then added ice.

She handed him his glass and as their fingertips brushed, he could swear he saw her shiver.

Okay, enough, he told himself. He shouldn't even be here. He should have stayed in his room and watched television.

Do what you came to do.

"I did a Google search on you," she said.

"You did?"

"I saw your back and I was curious. When my dad said you're a war hero, I thought he was exaggerating, but you actually *are* a hero."

He shrugged. "That's a matter of opinion."

"With a broken leg, you dragged a man from a burning helicopter. That's pretty brave, Colin."

"The truth is, I don't recall much of what happened. I remember getting caught in the sandstorm, the chopper going down. I recall being thrown and then looking back at the wreckage. I knew that William was probably still inside. I wasn't able to stand but being so jacked up on adrenaline, I didn't even know my leg was mangled. I dragged myself back to the chopper, felt around until I found him."

"There was smoke?"

He nodded. "Yeah, thick black smoke. And dust. Couldn't see a damn thing. I could hardly breathe. The explosion didn't happen until I had dragged him about twenty feet away. Then I passed out, but luckily William regained consciousness. He put out the fire on my back and then dragged me a safe distance away. When I woke up, I was in the hospital."

"And if you hadn't pulled him from the helicopter?"

"He would have burned to death. I was the only chance he had. He would have done the same for me. Easy choice. *No* choice, really."

"I read that he walked away with some burns and a broken arm."

"The burns were mostly on his hands and arms, from putting out the fire on me."

"He has a wife and four kids."

Colin nodded, acknowledging the unstated sentiment. "I know that people have labeled me a hero, but I don't see it that way. What I did for him, any other soldier would have done for me. It's just part of the job description."

"That doesn't make it any less heroic."

Not in his mind.

"Will you ever go back into active duty?"

"Never. With the damage to my leg I would be useless in combat. They gave me a choice. Take a desk job or retire. But I can't be an outsider looking in. I'm a warrior. Warriors don't sit behind desks."

"So what will you do now?"

"I have a friend in private security who offered me a job. The only thing holding me back is my leg."

"Does it still hurt?"

"Sometimes." Almost all the time, but not like before. Right after the surgery it was excruciating. He hadn't taken anything stronger than ibuprofen in a month.

"And your back?" she said.

"It's sensitive, but not painful."

"Can I...touch it?"

She was playing with fire. And who was more foolish—the fool who started the fire, or the fool who gave her the matches?

His gaze drifted down to her mouth, her lips full and pink and practically begging to be kissed. Then her tongue darted out to wet them....

Bloody hell. He had to stop this now.

"Rowena." He set his glass down. "We need to talk."

"Is something wrong?"

"I need to apologize for the other night. And this morning."

"Okay."

"I was very...forward the other night. I'm afraid I may have given you the wrong impression."

"Maybe a little," she admitted.

"And today...well, there's no excuse for my behavior. I was very rude to you. I'm sorry for that."

"But?"

"I like you, Rowena, but I *can't* like you."

"Is it my reputation? Are you worried it will tarnish your good name?"

"No! God no. Nothing like that. This is because of your father."

She frowned. "What about him?"

"After he introduced us, he and I had a talk. About you. And he warned me, in no uncertain terms, that I am to consider you off-limits."

Four

Rowena felt as if she'd been sucker-punched in the stomach.

The shock of Colin's words, her father's sheer gall, rendered her speechless. She honestly did not know what to say. And even if she did, her throat was so tight with anger, her vocal chords were frozen.

Her father controlled where she worked, where she lived, the decisions regarding her son's medical care. Now he wanted to control who she could see socially? What would be next? Her clothes? Her brand of shampoo? Would he keep going until he'd stolen every last shred of her independence?

For over three years now she had played by his rules, doing and saying what was expected of her, paying penance for her sins over and over. And he still wouldn't let go, wouldn't let her have a life of her own. What did she have to do to make him trust her? For him to see that she'd changed?

Or maybe all this time she had been wrong, maybe this had nothing to do with her proving herself, with him trusting her. Power hungry as he had always been, maybe it was simply that he liked to keep her firmly under his thumb, under his control.

In that moment, she resented the senator more than she ever believed possible.

"I think he's just worried about you," Colin said.

Her voice tight, Rowena replied, "Trust me, Colin, that's not it. Not at all."

"I'm so sorry," Colin said. "I can see that you're upset."

She took a deep, calming breath. "Let's get one thing very clear. Who I choose to see socially is *none* of my father's damn business."

"I don't think so either, but I can't risk him pulling his support for the treaty. We've come so far already."

"He said he would pull his support?"

"Not directly, but he insinuated it."

She was wrong—she actually *could* resent him more. She was so angry, so embarrassed and humiliated and disgusted—with her father and herself.

"Rowena?" He touched her shoulder. "Are you okay?"

She shook her head, brushing away an angry tear with the back of her hand. No. She wasn't okay. Her father had crossed the line. One he could never uncross. And the worst part was that she had let him.

But no more. This is where she drew *her* line. She was going to get away. She wasn't quite sure how, but she would figure it out. Her dignity and her pride depended on it. And it depended on something else.

"Colin, do you want to kiss me?"

He had this look, like maybe he thought it was a trick question.

"It's okay if you say no. I just want the truth."

"Yes, I do. But—"

"And I want you to. For the first time in over three years I met someone who I would like to kiss. I'll be damned if I'm going to let anyone, most of all my own father, tell me that I can't. No one else knows we're here, and I'm not going to tell anyone. So, if you really want to, just this one time, kiss me."

He stepped closer, his eyes locked on hers, and slid his hand through her hair to cradle the back of her head. Her heart pounded and her breath hitched as he leaned in, tilting her head....

Her eyes drifted closed as his lips brushed over hers. Once. Twice. More of a tease than anything. Then it was over.

He backed away, gazing down at her.

That's it? Seriously?

She didn't just want a kiss, she wanted a *kiss*.

"Colin, no offense, but I've waited over *three* years for this. Please tell me you can do better than that."

Maybe it was all that military training, or he was a ninja, but damn did he move fast. One second he was standing there looking at her, then she blinked and she was in his arms and he was kissing her. *Really* kissing her. And it was very much worth the wait.

She slid her arms around his neck, tunneled her fingers through his hair. Everything about him felt so solid and sturdy, but his touch, as he cradled her face in his hands and stroked her cheeks and ears, was so gentle.

He pulled away slowly this time, as if he knew he had to stop but didn't really want to. And as their lips finally parted, she felt limp and drowsy, as if she could melt into a puddle right there at his feet.

"How was that?" he asked.

She smiled up at him. "Thank you."

"I think that's the first time a woman has thanked me for kissing her. Though I'm not sure I deserved it."

"Why not?"

The corners of his lips tilted upward. "I think I can do better."

Better than that? She honestly didn't think it got any better than that. But if he thought he could, who was she to disagree?

"Okay, what's going on?"

Rowena looked up to find Tricia leaning in her office doorway. "What do you mean?"

"You haven't stopped smiling all day."

"I haven't?"

She shook her head.

She tried to wipe the smile from her face, but she couldn't do it. The corners of her mouth refused to drop.

"And it's a sappy, lovesick kind of smile," Tricia said. "There's obviously something you aren't telling me."

If she couldn't trust her best friend, who could she trust? "Close the door."

Tricia closed the door and sat expectantly on the edge of Rowena's desk. "Well?"

"You can't tell anyone about this."

"I won't, I swear. Did you meet someone?" She lowered her voice and in a raspy whisper asked, "Did you get laid?"

"Better," Rowena said. "I got kissed."

And kissed, and kissed, until she and Colin had both lost track of how many times. Until it hadn't even mattered anymore.

"Just a kiss?" Tricia said, looking disappointed.

"Yep."

"You didn't do anything else?"

"Nope. We just kissed. But it wasn't *just* kissing. It was

like…high school. That perfect first kiss in the backseat of a car, the kind where you're so into each other that everything around you just…goes away. You lose track of time, of where you are and *who* you are. It was…perfect."

"Wow," Tricia said, a dreamy look on her face. "I want a kiss like that."

"It was a slice of heaven."

"You have to tell me who it is and how you met him. Did you meet him on the internet? People do that a lot now."

Rowena laughed. "Nope. Not the internet."

"Then who—"

A knock cut her short. Tricia pulled the door open and Rowena was stunned to see Colin standing on the other side. He wore jogging pants and a sweat-soaked jersey, and boy, did he wear them well. Her heart skipped a beat and her face went hot.

"Colin…hi," she said, wondering what he was doing there, and even more importantly, why he would risk getting caught.

"Have you got a minute?" he asked.

"Um, yeah, sure. Tricia, would you excuse us?"

Tricia looked from Colin to her, and that was all she needed to make the connection.

"Sure." Colin stepped into the room and Tricia stepped out, and when his back was to her, she mouthed the words, *oh, my God,* and fanned her face.

When the door latched, Rowena asked him, "What are you doing here? What if someone saw you?"

"Your father had a late lunch meeting, and I decided to go jogging. If anyone asks, I'll say I stopped in for a glass of water."

"Wooter?" she teased. "I'm not sure if we have any of that."

His brow lifted, lips curled into a grin. "Making fun of my acccnt, are we?"

Honestly, every time he talked, it gave her warm shivers. She could listen to him for hours and never get bored. But that was beside the point. "Colin, you can't be here. We said it was just going to be that one time."

"And I haven't stopped thinking about you since then."

"Please don't say things like that." It made her go all gooey inside. Like last night, when she had to go, and he kept saying, *No, not yet, just one more kiss.*

Who could say no to that? But this time she had to. "You only want me because you can't have me."

"That's not true," he said, and she raised her brows at him. "Okay, it's a little true. What can I say? I'm a thrill seeker. I like to live dangerously. I crave adventure."

"Colin, if I said yes and we were caught—"

"We won't be."

"But if we were I would feel awful."

"Rowena—"

Another knock cut him off, but this was louder and more urgent. "It's me, Row," Tricia called. "We need you."

"So open the door."

Tricia opened it, peeking in like she expected them to be half naked. "There was an incident on the playground."

Rowena was instantly up and out of her chair, brushing past Colin to get to the door.

"Now don't freak out," the woman said. "There was a *minor* accident."

"Who?"

"It's nothing too serious. Maybe he'll need a few stitches—"

"Tricia, *who?*"

"Dylan, but—"

Rowena was already out the door, and Colin could swear as she ran, her feet never once touched the ground.

Colin followed them. Having been trained as a combat medic, he could potentially be of help.

"By the way, I'm Tricia Adams," the woman walking beside him said.

"Colin Middlebury," he said as they half walked, half ran after Rowena. Sitting on the playground near one of the wooden structures was a girl who couldn't have been older than eighteen. Cradled in her lap was a young boy, thin, pale and fragile-looking, with unruly reddish-blond hair and big expressive eyes. If he hadn't known he was Rowena's son, the eyes and hair would have been a dead giveaway.

The girl held a blood-spotted cloth against his head, but he wasn't crying and didn't even look distressed.

"What happened?" Rowena demanded, scooping her son out of the girl's arms. She gently lifted the cloth and examined the wound.

"He tripped and went headfirst into the monkey bars," Tricia said.

"He was running?"

Tricia nodded.

Rowena tilted her son's chin up, looked him in the eye and in a calm but firm tone said, "Dylan, what have I told you about running on the playground?"

The boy's lower lip curled into a pout and he shrugged.

"Are you supposed to run on the playground?"

His lower lip beginning to quiver, he shook his head.

"And why do I tell you not to run?"

"I could faw," he said in a small and wobbly voice. Colin knew practically nothing about kids, but he was guessing that this one couldn't be much older than two.

"But you ran anyway," Rowena said. "And what happened?"

"I fawed."

"And you got hurt, didn't you?"

He nodded.

"Next time will you listen to Mommy?"

He nodded again, and Colin couldn't help feeling sorry for him. She could at least give him a hug or a kiss or *something* to soothe him.

Rowena turned to Tricia. "It looks as if this will need a stitch or two. Can you handle things while I drive him to the hospital?"

When he heard the word "hospital," Dylan's eyes went wide and he started to squirm in his mother's arms, shrieking, "No! No hobspital, Mommy!"

"But you have a bad boo-boo, sweetie. You need to see a doctor."

He began crying in earnest, struggling and screaming, "No! No dopter! No hobspital!"

For whatever reason, he was clearly terrified. Colin wondered if the wound was really so bad that it needed stitches.

"Can I have a look?" he said.

Rowena turned to him, blinking in surprise, as if she hadn't even realized he was there. Then she frowned and held Dylan closer. "Why?"

"I trained as a medic. I've seen every sort of wound there is. He may not need stitches. Or a hospital."

Hearing that, Dylan instantly stopped fussing and looked up at Colin, eyes wide and full of hope. Rowena asked her son, "Is that okay, sweetie? Can Mr. Middlbury look at your boo-boo?"

Eyes narrowed with suspicion, he asked Colin, "You a dopter?"

"Not exactly," Colin said, approaching him cautiously. "But I do know how to help people who are hurt. Will you let me see?"

Dylan hesitated, then nodded.

Colin tilted his head down and gently parted Dylan's blood-matted hair to inspect the wound. Dylan had a small gash just above his hairline, barely more than a quarter inch long, and though the bleeding had stopped, it was awfully deep.

"Does it hurt?" he asked Dylan, who shrugged.

To leave it open would be risking infection. A stitch or two would do the trick, but the child was already traumatized. Fortunately, during his training, Colin had learned a few tricks.

"I don't think he'll need stitches," he told Rowena, and she looked at him as if he'd lost his mind.

"It's not as if we can butterfly it closed with his hair in the way. It's a gaping…" She paused, censoring herself. "It's *d-e-e-p*."

Dylan's mop of hair was the very reason they would be able to close the wound. "Do you have a first-aid kit?"

"Of course, but—"

"Have a little faith, Rowena."

She opened her mouth to argue, and Colin said, "Do you want him even more traumatized, or will you at least let me try?"

Conflicted, she looked down at her son, and for a moment Colin was sure she would say no and drag the boy kicking and screaming to the nearest medical facility. But after several seconds she said, "Okay, you can try, as long as you don't hurt him."

As if he would purposely try to hurt the boy. "First we need to wash it out."

"Bathroom sink?" she said.

He nodded and followed Rowena into the building. "Why don't you sit with him in your lap and wrap your arms around him to hold him still?"

She closed the toilet lid and sat down with Dylan in her lap. Tricia handed Colin the first-aid kit.

Colin rummaged through it, setting everything he needed on the edge of the sink, then told Dylan, "I have to clean this, and it might sting a little, but if you hold very still, you won't have to go to the hospital."

Eyes wide and full of relief, Dylan sat absolutely still as Colin rinsed the cut thoroughly, and as he applied the antiseptic, the child barely even flinched.

"You're being so brave," Rowena said, giving her son a squeeze and a kiss on the cheek.

"Okay, now you have to hold very, very still," he told Dylan, grabbing the tweezers and dipping them in antiseptic. He very gently used them to separate a few strands of hair from each side of the wound. Though it took several tries, he managed to tie the strands together in a firm knot, essentially using the hair as a stitch.

Tricia laughed and said, "That's *genius!*"

"But it only works on hair that's long enough." If Dylan's hair were a quarter of an inch shorter, Rowena would probably be taking him to the E.R.

It only required two knots to seal the wound, and then Colin dabbed the area with liquid bandage to hold everything in place and keep any dirt or moisture out.

"Good as new," he told Dylan, gently ruffling the back of his hair. "Did it hurt?"

Dylan held his thumb and finger a centimeter or so apart to indicate that it had only hurt a little. Then he looked at Rowena and said excitedly, "No hobspital?"

She smiled and said, "No, baby, no hospital."

"You'll want to keep that dry for a few days, give it a chance to close."

"He had a bath this morning, so he should be fine for now. Or maybe he'll just have a stinky head," she teased, tickling Dylan under the ribs. He giggled and squirmed in her lap.

"Tinky head, tinky head," he chanted, as if that were the funniest thing he'd ever heard. And being that he was so young, it just might have been. But at least he was happy now.

"Can you tell Colin thank you?" Rowena said.

"Hubs!" Dylan held out his arms, and as Rowena handed him over, Colin realized that he wanted *hugs*. Dylan wrapped his arms around Colin's neck, and for such a small, fragile-looking kid, he had one hell of a grip. Though Dylan obviously had a speech impediment, when he said "thank you" the words were perfectly clear, and when he planted a big wet kiss on Colin's cheek, his heart melted. He sure was a sweet kid, and seemed exceptionally smart for such a little guy.

Colin handed Dylan back to Rowena and she said, "After all that excitement, I think someone could use a nap."

Dylan turned to Colin, flashing a thousand-watt smile, and said, "Cowin tuck me in?"

Five

It would seem as though Colin had earned himself a new friend. Rowena shot him a questioning look.

Odds were good someone would see him walking them into the house, but weren't these extenuating circumstances? What sort of man would he be if he told the boy no?

"I'll tuck you in," Colin said.

"Are you sure?" Rowena asked.

"Of course."

"Okay, then." She turned to Tricia. "I'll probably be out for the rest of the day. Can you manage without me?"

"We have four kids out with the flu. We should be fine."

"Go grab your backpack," Rowena said, setting Dylan down. As Colin watched him make his way across the room, he realized why running on the playground—or anywhere else—was so frowned upon. Rather than walk like a typical toddler, Dylan hobbled along unsteadily, balancing on the sides of his feet, looking as though any second he could topple over. Colin could relate. He'd spent the first eight weeks after his surgery hobbling around on crutches. But as the doctor had said, he was lucky to have a leg to walk on.

Dylan hobbled back over, but when Rowena leaned down to pick him up he said, "No. *Cowin* take me."

Rowena looked over at him, mouthing the word "sorry," but he honestly didn't mind. Dylan held out his arms and Colin lifted him up. He was heavier and sturdier than he looked. By the time they made it all the way up the path to the mansion and up to Rowena's suite, his arms were getting tired.

The greater part of the senator's mansion was about as warm and welcoming as a museum, and far too gaudy for Colin's taste. Too much gold and beige and useless excess. In contrast, Rowena and Dylan's suite was an explosion of color. It was casually furnished with an eclectic mix of antique and modern, all in bold prints and colorful patterns, yet the kitchen was ultramodern, with polished marble counters and stainless steel appliances. Nothing seemed to match, yet it all fit in perfectly together, and though it was very clean, it had a comfortable, lived-in look.

Rowena obviously did a fair share of reading. Wall-to-wall built-in bookcases crammed full of hardbacks, paperbacks and magazines bordered a picture window with a padded window seat, where he could just imagine her curled up with a book or reading Dylan a story. Everything about the room seemed to suit her somehow.

"Dylan's room is this way," she said, and he followed her down a short hall where nearly every square inch of the walls was covered with photos of her son. They started at birth—a time during which he clearly had serious health problems—and ranged to much more recent photos. In those, Dylan was always smiling, always looked happy.

Colin couldn't help noticing, though, that in all the photos, something important was missing. Dylan's father.

Had there been a bitter divorce? A falling-out? Or was he simply not a part of his son's life?

Across the hall from Dylan's room was what had to be Rowena's bedroom. He could see through the open door that it was decorated in soft, warm colors, and he recognized the girly scents drifting out.

Rowena led him into Dylan's room to his crib.

"At the risk of sounding like a novice, what's routine when tucking in a child?" Colin asked her.

"Colin needs your help, Dylan," she said. "Tell him what to do."

"Hubs!" Dylan shrieked, wrapping his arms around Colin's neck, giving him another one of those firm squeezes. He couldn't remember ever being embraced with such enthusiasm or genuine affection in his whole life.

"Cwib."

Colin lowered him into the crib and Dylan sat awkwardly, then lay back against the pillow. "Cubbers!"

Cubbers? Colin looked to Rowena for a translation.

She nodded to the blanket hanging over the side rail. *Covers.* Of course. Colin didn't want to be responsible for the kid catching cold and maybe coming down with pneumonia.

He pulled the blanket down over Dylan. "How's that?"

"Good!" Dylan said, but obviously not good enough, because as Rowena bent over to kiss him, she tucked the blanket even higher up under his chin.

"Does your boo-boo hurt?" she asked, and Dylan shook his head.

"Sawee, Mommy."

"It's okay, just go to sleep."

They stepped out of Dylan's room and Rowena shut the

door behind her. She leaned against it and dropped her head in her hands, saying softly, "I'm a terrible mother."

"You are not a terrible mother," Colin said, but Rowena sure felt like one.

"My baby hurts himself, and the first thing I do when I see him is *scold* him? What kind of a parent does that?"

"Why don't we go sit on the sofa so Dylan can sleep?"

She nodded and they walked into the living room. He sat down on the sofa, patting the cushion beside him, and when she sat, he took her hand. There was nothing suggestive or sexual about it, it was just very…comforting. And though she knew that the last thing he probably wanted was to sit there and listen to her silly insecurities, the words just sort of rolled off her tongue on their own. "I'm scared to death that Dylan will grow up to hate me."

"No, he won't. He obviously adores you."

"But I made him feel even worse."

"I'm sure that by the time he wakes up he'll have forgotten all about it."

She shook her head. "You don't know Dylan. He remembers *everything*."

"Well, then, he must have remembered that he wasn't supposed to run. Right?"

"He's just a little boy. I know that I'm too hard on him sometimes."

"Rowena, listen to me. You were scared, and you overreacted a little. Kids are resilient. I know because I was one."

Being a kid and having one relying on you for everything were two very different things. And sometimes it was so hard doing it all alone. But Colin was not the man she should be pouring her heart out to.

"I'm sorry to have dragged you into this."

He looked confused. "Into what?"

"This whole—" she gestured randomly "—domestic scenario. I know that's the last thing you want to be dealing with. I didn't even intend to introduce you to Dylan."

"Why? I'm happy to have met him. He seems like a very special boy."

"Thank you for what you did."

"Dylan obviously hates going to the hospital. I take it from the photos in the hall that he's spent considerable time there."

"He was born with cerebral palsy, and yes, he was in the hospital a lot when he was a baby. The doctors told me he might never walk, and that he would probably be mentally disabled. I didn't listen. I made it my mission to prove them wrong. He's light-years from where he was when he was first born, but that's only because I work with him constantly. With his speech problems, people sometimes think he's slow."

"I thought he seemed exceptionally bright."

"He is. He didn't start walking unaided until he was two, but he started to speak in two- and three-word sentences before his first birthday."

"How old is he now?"

"Two and a half."

"He's very smart for his age."

"Sometimes he's a little too smart for his own good. And he tries to do more than he should, like running."

"Well, he's okay now," Colin said.

"He's okay now, but what about the next time?" she said.

"You just can't think about that."

"But I do. Constantly. I'm always on edge, always waiting for the other shoe to drop. For something really horrible to happen. He's so small and fragile."

"That isn't want I see when I look at him."

That surprised her. "No?"

"I see a kid who's had it rough, but doesn't let it slow him down. How many kids his age would take a tumble and hurt themselves, and not even cry?"

"He's been through much worse."

"Exactly. And I'm guessing that he just wants to be like the other kids, wants to be a normal little boy."

"But he's not."

"That's not the point."

Was he trying to confuse her? "What is the point?"

"It isn't how *you* see him, or anyone else, for that matter. It's how he sees himself. I have scars all over my back, and titanium holding my left leg together, and yes, it's limited me physically, but I'm still me. Who I am inside hasn't changed."

"Yeah, but Dylan's health is in constant flux. Just recently he started having seizures. At first I was afraid to leave him for a second. When Tricia first came to get me, that's what I assumed had happened."

"Obviously it wasn't."

"No, which means the medication he's on seems to be working. And his neurologist believes it's something that he'll outgrow."

"That's encouraging. As far as his other disabilities go, what's his prognosis?"

"Well, he'll never be completely steady on his feet, and will need occasional surgeries to lengthen the tendons in his ankles. His compromised immune system will always make him susceptible to certain illnesses. But if he eats well and takes care of himself, there's no reason why he won't lead a long and productive life. But it won't always be easy for him. He'll have to work harder than the average person."

"Everyone has their cross to bear. We all have challenges. Like I said before, it's all about accepting who you are. If you accept Dylan the way he is, he'll learn to accept himself."

She hoped so. "I know I've already said this, but thank you. I don't even want to think about what I'd be doing right now, and putting Dylan through, if it wasn't for you."

Colin stroked her palm with his thumb and moved a little closer. "I know a way you could show your appreciation."

"Colin…"

The protest died in her throat as he leveled that piercing gaze on her, flashed her a coaxing smile. "You know you want to. And we're already here. Alone. Seems a shame to waste the opportunity."

"You're not playing fair," she said, but she was already leaning in, anticipating the touch of his lips.

"Do I honestly strike you as the type to play fair?" he said, pulling her into his lap.

"Okay, but this is *definitely* the last time."

Six

Colin cupped Rowena's face in his hands and kissed her… and kissed her…and *kissed* her. But just like last night, he kept his hands in the safe zones, and so did she. The shoulders, the face. The middle of the back. And now she was thinking, if this was going to be the last time, maybe they could do a little more touching. Nothing too racy of course, just some on-top-of-the-clothes stuff.

Thinking that maybe she could get the ball rolling, she let her hand very casually slide from his shoulder down to his chest. His body heat seeped through his nylon shirt and she could feel the heavy thud of his heart.

Colin's hand, which had been resting on her back just above her hip, suddenly went missing in action. Thinking he had taken the hint, she waited, heart pounding in anticipation, breath coming faster…then shuddering to an abrupt halt when his hand settled over hers, lifted it from his chest and set it back on his shoulder.

Okay, so maybe he hadn't gotten the hint.

She waited a minute or so, so as not to appear too forward or, for that matter, desperate. But this time she only got as far as caressing the top of his pec before he intercepted her hand and he stopped kissing her.

Well, shoot.

"Not a good idea," he said, wrapping his hand around hers and holding it.

"What if I think it is?"

"I'm exercising a tremendous amount of self-control. You ought not to tempt me."

The look in his eyes said he wasn't exaggerating. She just assumed that like her, he was content with kissing, but clearly he wanted more. Which made her even hotter for him.

If he wasn't going to play fair, then neither was she.

With her eyes locked on his, using her free hand, she slid her index finger down the center of his chest, over his rock hard abs, all the way to the waist of his pants. She started back up, but barely made it halfway before he pulled a ninja move on her again. One second she was in his lap, then next she was flat on her back on the sofa cushions, Colin grinning down at her.

"I warned you."

She slid her arms around his neck, pulled him down and kissed him. He settled on top of her and slightly to the left, and—*well, hello there.* There was definitely no denying that he wanted her, too.

She forgot how much she loved this, the steady pressure of a man's weight pressing her into the mattress—or in this case, the sofa. It was one of a thousand little things about sex that she loved, but had completely forgotten.

"Can I take off your shirt?" she said.

He grinned down at her. "I don't know, can you?"

She grabbed the bottom edge and pulled it up, and Colin helped her pull it over his head.

"I love looking at you," she said, flattening her palms against his chest. "And touching you." She pulled his head back down. "And kissing you."

Her cell phone started to ring and she ignored it.

"Should you answer that?" Colin asked.

Hell no. She was fooling around for the first time in more than *three* years. Nothing was going to interrupt them. "They can leave a message. Kiss me."

With a grin he kissed her, and eventually the ringing stopped. Then started right back up again. Seriously? It had to be right now? They couldn't call her back later?

"Maybe you should get that," Colin said. "It could be important."

The only thing worth stopping for would be Dylan, and he was asleep, safe and sound in his crib. "They can call back later."

"Are you sure?"

She nodded, pulling him back down. "Just keep kissing me."

She tuned out the ringing, blocked out everything but Colin. The feel of his mouth…on her lips and her neck. The taste of his skin and mingling scents of soap and sweat.

When her damned phone started to ring *again,* Colin stopped kissing her and said, "I really think you should answer that."

She mumbled a curse and dug her phone out of her back pocket. It was Tricia. "Somebody had better be dead."

"I'm sorry to bother you. I just thought you might like to know that the senator is coming to see you."

"What? *Why?*"

"He came down here to talk to you and one of the girls

told him what happened to Dylan. He's on his way up to see if he's okay."

Damn, damn, *damn*. "Thanks for the heads-up."

"So," Tricia said, in a tone dripping with innuendo. "How's it going?"

The fact that Rowena hadn't answered her phone should have been a clue. "I'll call you later."

Muttering a word that was very unladylike, she hung up and tossed her phone on the coffee table. Pushing on Colin's chest, she said, "Up, up, up. Time to get up."

He pushed himself off her. "What's wrong?"

She bolted up from the sofa. "My father heard what happened and is on his way up to check on Dylan."

"Are you serious?"

She grabbed his shirt off the floor and tossed it to him. "I'm assuming you probably don't want to be here when he shows up."

He pulled it on. "Preferably not."

She wondered how long they had before he got there. Her answer came about ten seconds later when he knocked.

"Okay, now what?" Colin said.

"My bedroom," she said, pushing him in that direction. "I'll call you when the coast is clear."

Her father knocked again. The second Colin closed the bedroom door, she opened the suite door, pretending to be surprised to see him. "Hello, Father."

He muscled his way inside and demanded, "Where's Dylan?"

Deep breaths, in and out. "He's napping."

"Why didn't you call me and tell me what happened?"

"Dylan falling, you mean?" She shrugged. "He's fine."

"They told me he was bleeding," he said, looking around suspiciously, obviously not for his grandson, since she had just told him Dylan was in bed.

"He hit his head, but he is fine," she told him.

"And Colin?" her father asked.

She feigned confusion. "What about him?"

"They said he came back to the house with you."

"Dylan wanted Colin to tuck him in."

"And?"

"And…he did."

"Why was he even at the day-care center?"

"He was jogging past and stopped when he heard Dylan crying. He thought he could help. He said something about being a medic in the navy."

"Royal army," the senator corrected her.

She shrugged, as if it made no difference to her one way or the other. "He fixed Dylan up, then walked us home."

"Where is he now?"

"I don't know. As soon as Dylan was down for his nap, Colin left." She paused and asked, "Why? Were you expecting me to entertain him for the rest of the afternoon?"

"Of course not."

"Did you want me to call you when Dylan wakes up?"

"I'll be out for the evening. I'll see him tomorrow at breakfast."

Which meant he was less concerned about his grandson than if Colin was in her room. Great to know.

She walked him to the door.

"Did you fill out an accident report?" he asked.

"Are you worried that I'm going to sue you?"

He gave her the *look*. Maybe he *was* worried. Maybe he *should* be.

"I'll fill one out tomorrow."

He left and she shut the door, leaning against it. She waited another minute or so, then said, "Coast is clear."

Colin stepped out of her bedroom.

"Sorry about that."

"That's all right. I kept myself busy going through your things."

She shot him a look.

"I was actually listening at the door. Very nice save when he asked why I was at the day care, by the way."

She collapsed on the couch, suddenly exhausted. "I thought it was more plausible than you getting a glass of water."

Colin sat down beside her, a good foot away. "He sounded suspicious."

"Yeah, well, he pretty much always sounds like that. With me, anyway. If he really thought you were here, he would have searched the entire apartment. I'd say you have nothing to worry about."

"That's a relief."

She looked over at the clock. "Dylan should be waking up soon."

He nodded. "So I guess that's it."

"I guess so. This is probably going to sound juvenile, but thank you for this. It really meant a lot to me. And not just in a sexual way. For a really long time, I haven't felt like myself. The truth is, I completely lost track of who I even am. But now, after this…I kinda feel a little bit like my old self again. I've needed to make some changes in my life, and now, I think I'm ready."

"I'm not sure what I did, but I'm glad I could help."

She walked to the door and he followed her. "I guess I'll probably see you around."

"I'm sure you will."

She pushed up on her toes to kiss his cheek, because if she kissed his lips, even for a second, she wouldn't want to stop. Then she opened the door and he walked out. Simple, uncomplicated and dignified. If every break-up could be so easy. But after two days and a little bit of passionate kissing, what did she expect? That sort of thing probably happened to Colin all the time.

She grabbed her laptop from the kitchen on her way back to the sofa, and sat with her legs curled beneath her.

Feeling truly brave for the first time in ages, she opened her computer, clicked on the browser and typed in the address for the Los Angeles Department of Health Services.

This, she decided, would be the official first day of her new life.

The following Monday, Rowena welcomed a new addition to the day-care family. Matt was an adorable blond-haired, blue-eyed six-week-old whose mother had just finished her maternity leave. It was always exciting to have a new baby around, especially one so young, and for the first hour he was a total angel. Then he began to scream, and hadn't stopped for more than five minutes all day. Everyone took turns rocking, changing, feeding and burping him, but no matter what they tried, he wouldn't settle.

It wasn't uncommon for a baby to be upset his first day away from his mommy, so Rowena figured the next day would be easier. It wasn't. The poor little guy was inconsolable, and by afternoon everyone had reached the limit of their patience. At quiet time, when the bigger kids did their homework and the smaller ones napped, Rowena locked herself in her office with Matt so the near-constant howling wouldn't agitate the other children.

Quiet time was only half over when Tricia knocked on her office door and poked her head in. "Hey, you've got a guest."

Since her father was the only "guest" she ever had, she assumed it was him. With a sigh, she said, "Send him in."

She quit the solitaire game she had been playing on her computer, since trying to concentrate on anything with an infant screaming in her ear was impossible, and when she heard the door open again, looked up, expecting the senator. *"Colin?"*

"Hello," he said, with a smile that made her go instantly gooey, like the smooth caramel center of her favorite candy bar. "Have you got a minute?"

She'd spent the past four days doing her best not to think about him. And not very successfully.

"Um…sure," she said. "Just shut the door behind you."

He shot her a questioning look.

"So Matt here doesn't disrupt quiet time."

"Ahhh," he said. He stepped inside and closed the door.

"What are you doing here?" she asked.

"I wanted to check in and see how Dylan was healing," he said, loud enough to be heard over Matt's screams.

"Great! He's been telling everyone who will listen how you saved him from the evil hospital."

"How have you been?" he asked.

"Good," she said, wondering if she was the only one who noticed how stilted and awkward this conversation sounded. She really wished that he would stay on his own side of the fence. But she didn't want to be rude. "And yourself?"

"Busy. We've made quite a bit of progress. Though we still have a long way to go."

"I'm glad to hear that it's going well." The sooner he went back to England, the better off she would be. In a God-my-life-is-pathetically-boring way. But for now that was about all she could handle.

Matt let out a particularly high-pitched shriek, and Colin cringed. "Is he all right?"

"He's new to the day care and missing his mommy. With any luck he'll calm down after a day or two. Although sometimes it takes weeks. We all take turns holding him."

"It's your turn?"

"Just while the others are resting." Her arm was getting tired, so she moved Matt to the opposite shoulder. She heard a loud, juicy belch, then felt something warm and wet down her back. Then Matt went right back to crying.

"Sounds like someone left you a present," Colin said.

Felt like it, too. She rose from the chair and turned. "How bad is it?"

"Well, have you got another shirt to change into?"

She did. She kept a few spares, for occasions such as this. She looked around for a good place to temporarily lay Matt down, but there didn't seem to be one.

"Shall I have a go at it while you change?" he said, holding out his arms.

He seriously did not look like the type to handle a crying infant. "Are you sure? It's ear piercing."

"Have you ever heard a mortar detonate at close range?" he asked.

Good point. She handed Matt over, her fingers brushing Colin's in the process. Amazing how the simplest touch could get her pulse jumping.

Colin turned Matt a bit awkwardly until the baby was propped comfortably on his shoulder. Matt hiccuped out one more pathetic cry, exhaled a shuddering breath, then went silent.

What the hell?

"What did you do?" Rowena asked.

Colin stood stock still, as if the slightest movement might jinx it. "I don't know. Is he still breathing?"

She took a look. "He's fine, just sleeping."

Honestly, it probably had more to do with that burp than anything Colin was doing, but hey, whatever worked.

"I'll be back in a minute." She grabbed one of the spare shirts from her bottom desk drawer and darted off to the bathroom. When she got back to her office a few minutes later, Matt was still sleeping.

"Thanks," she said, taking him, but the second the baby was back in her arms he started to cry. It was probably just a coincidence, but she asked Colin, "Let's try that again."

Colin took Matt and the crying stopped. She took him back, and he fussed.

Okay, no way was that a coincidence.

"I think he likes me," Colin said.

"So do I."

One brow tipped up. "You like me, too?"

"I meant—" She shook her head and laughed. "Never mind. Most infants prefer a woman's touch, but there are some who seem to respond better to men."

"Would you like me to hold him for a while? Give your employees a break?"

She had not expected that. "You wouldn't mind?"

"I've nothing to do between now and dinner."

"And if my father should make a surprise visit?"

"Covered. He thanked me the other day for helping, and I mentioned stopping by to see Dylan."

"So you've been planning this for days?"

"It never hurts to be prepared."

"I do have to get the payroll information sent out today by five, or come next Friday I'm going to have some very unhappy employees. Technically, since you don't work here, I shouldn't let you, but I doubt Matt's mother would mind." Hell, one look at him holding Matt and she would probably melt.

He gave the baby a stiff sideways glance, as if he feared the slightest movement might jostle Matt awake. "What should I do? Just stand here?"

She certainly didn't want him hovering there looking over her shoulder while she worked. Even while cuddling an infant, he radiated too much pure testosterone, was too much *man* for the small office. "Why don't you try sitting in the rocker in the infants' room and see how that goes?"

"I'll give it a shot," he said, easing his way out the door.

She listened for several minutes, but could only hear the sounds of the other children waking up from their naps and preparing for the afternoon snack. No infant screams or fussing.

She finished her paperwork, and after emailing everything to the payroll company, she made her way into the playroom. It had been a while, so she wouldn't have been surprised to find that Colin had grown bored and had probably passed Matt off to one of the girls, but as she walked into the infant room, there he was in the rocker, Matt limp against his chest. If that wasn't adorable enough, Dylan sat on his lap, cuddling close to both Colin and the baby. In Colin's hand was a beat-up copy of *The Velveteen Rabbit* that one of the parents had donated, and he was reading it in a low and steady voice.

It was such a touching scene, and so exactly what Dylan needed, that for a full two or three minutes she just stood there watching with a pinch in her heart so intense it was difficult to breathe. For all the love she had given Dylan and the attention she'd lavished on him, it could never make up for the hole his father had left in his life.

"It melts your heart, doesn't it?" Tricia whispered from behind her.

Without taking her eyes off them, Rowena nodded.

"Dylan has really taken to Colin, and Colin is so good with him. They're like best buds."

Rowena turned to her. "Don't do that."

"What?" Tricia said, shrugging innocently, when she knew damn well what Rowena meant.

"He's not the settling-down type."

"Statistically speaking, he will settle down at some point. It could be with you."

"I don't want that right now. And even if I did, it would be a logistical nightmare. With Colin's home in England, and all of Dylan's doctors and therapists here in California, it would never work."

"What are you girls whispering about?" Colin said, grinning at the two of them.

"Work stuff," Tricia lied, but Colin's look said he was skeptical.

"Mommy!" Dylan said in a loud whisper. "Cowin wead to me."

"I see that," Rowena said softly, stepping into the room.

"I haven't read this since I was a child," Colin said. "It used to be one of my favorites."

"You look as if you have your hands full. Why don't I take Matt? He's due for a bottle soon."

As Colin handed him over, Matt startled awake and started to cry. She carried him into the kitchen to grab a bottle, but when she sat down and tried to feed him, he kept spitting the nipple out. She changed his diaper, but it was barely wet. She put him over her shoulder to pat his back—careful to use a burp cloth this time—and he cried even harder, until he was nearly hysterical. She finally gave up and carried him back into the infant room, where Colin and Dylan still sat.

"Baby Matt cwyin'," Dylan said.

"Yes, sweetheart. He is one unhappy little boy."

"Not having any luck?" Colin said.

"Could you try holding him again?"

He nodded. "I'll give it a go."

She handed him back, and the instant Matt settled on Colin's shoulder, the crying miraculously stopped.

Rowena laughed and shook her head. This was clearly no fluke.

"His mom should be picking him up around six. Are you okay holding him for another forty minutes or so?"

"If you could grab us a couple more books."

It was the *least* she could do. She went into the other room to the bookcase and picked out a few of Dylan's favorites.

"Thanks," he said when she handed them to him.

"Wead to me, Cowin!" Dylan pleaded, squirming restlessly in Colin's lap. "Pweeze!"

"Hold on a second, bud." He looked up at Rowena and said, "Did you know that the senator left for Northern California this afternoon?"

Her pulse jumped and she couldn't help thinking, *oh no, here we go again.* "He never mentioned it, no."

"He won't be back until late tomorrow morning."

Why was he doing this to her?

"Probably going to be a nice night for a swim."

She had been at the pool swimming laps every night, half hoping, half dreading that she might look over and find him lying in his chair—she would never think of it as anything but *his* from now on—but he never was. And as much as she wanted him—and boy, did she want him— it was still a bad idea.

Seven

Rowena had debated going to the pool all evening. On one hand, she didn't want to tempt herself. On the other hand, she did her laps every night. If Colin did show up, she could still tell him no.

When Betty arrived at nine to watch Dylan, Rowena headed down to the pool, telling herself that no matter what happened, no matter what he said, she would put her foot down this time. She would insist they keep their relationship platonic. But when she got there, he wasn't in the chair.

Despite her internal pep talk, her heart sank. Clearly he'd had time to think about it, and he, too, decided it was better for everyone if they didn't—

She gasped as a pair of hands settled on her waist.

He leaned so close she could feel his breath on the shell of her ear. "You didn't throw me into the pool this time."

She probably should have. "Colin—"

"No one saw me leave."

"So it's okay as long as we don't get caught?"

"Can you give me another reason why we shouldn't? Just one."

She opened her mouth to recite an entire laundry list of reasons. And drew a complete blank.

"Can't do it, can you?"

She hated that he was right.

"And it's just going to be this one last time," she said, turning to him. "I don't care if my father goes on a month-long African safari. When we walk away from this pool tonight, it's over."

"Well, then, let's not waste another minute," he said, taking her hand and leading her to the pool house. She unlocked the door and let them in, but instead of turning on the lights, she made her way through the dark kitchen for the emergency candles and matches. Lamplight could draw attention, but no one would see the dim glow of candles, and there was the added bonus of it being romantic.

She lit a candle and set it on the coffee table, then opened the cedar chest, where they kept sheets and blankets for the fold-out couch. She grabbed one of the thickest and softest in the pile and spread it out on the floor.

"Doesn't the couch fold out?" Colin asked.

"Yes, but it's miserably uncomfortable."

"Done this before, have we?" he said, sounding amused.

She looked over at him and grinned. "My friends used to call it the love shack."

In the candlelight, dressed all in black, Colin looked sexy and edgy and maybe even a little dangerous.

He kicked off his shoes and walked over to where she stood, unbuttoning his shirt, his eyes raking over her. "What's under the cover-up tonight?"

That was going to take a little explaining. "Okay, you have to promise not to be smug."

His brows rose.

"Plan number one was to come down here, tell you we couldn't do this, then go back home. And if that didn't pan out, I came up with plan number two."

"Which is…?"

"Save as much time as possible getting to the good part." She grabbed the hem of the garment and pulled it over her head. The sound he made, the look of red-hot desire in his eyes when he realized what she was—or more to the point, *wasn't*—wearing underneath warmed her blood.

He mumbled a curse. "I guess that answers my next question."

"What's that?"

"Exactly how far you were expecting this to go."

"All the way."

His eyes raked over her. "You have an amazing body."

"It's a bit curvier than it was before I had Dylan," she said.

"Your curves are what I like," he said, reaching up to trace the underside of one breast, then the other. "I prefer women to actually look like women, not adolescent boys."

Well, that was good, she supposed. Because if adolescent boys were his thing, that would be a problem.

He pulled his shirt off and tossed it onto the couch. Talk about an amazing body. She touched him, sliding her hands up his wide chest and across his strong shoulders. She'd completely forgotten about his scars until her fingers brushed his back and she felt the uneven texture where he'd healed. It was warm and deceptively soft.

"Does it hurt when I touch you here?" she asked.

He shook his head. "It feels nice."

"How about here?" She rubbed her hand across the fly of his pants, squeezing his erection through the fabric and felt it growing longer and thicker in her hand.

Colin closed his eyes. "That's nice, as well."

She unfastened his pants and pushed them down. Colin kicked them away, then dipped his head, teasing her nipple with his tongue, sucking it into his mouth. It had been so long since a man had touched her, he could blow raspberries on her belly and it would feel erotic. But this was so much better. He gave the opposite breast the same attention, then sank to his knees. She held her breath as he kissed his way downward, thinking, *Please, please, please.*

In her experience, it was a rare man who liked to perform oral sex, and only a handful who were good at it. But when it came to receiving it, she'd never once met a man who said, "No, thank you, just not my thing." So when Colin sank lower, as his fingers parted her and his tongue darted out to taste her, the neglected, sex-starved woman in her shouted, *Yes!* Or maybe she said it out loud, because one second she was standing, and the next, her back was hitting the floor. And this must have been her lucky day because he was *really* good at it.

Almost too good. Pleasure crept up on her, quiet and stealthy, like a wild animal stalking its prey; then it pounced, suddenly and violently, driving its claws and teeth into skin and muscle and even bone.

When she opened her eyes Colin was grinning down at her. "Are you always this easy to bring off?"

"It's been a long time since I've been with anyone," she said breathlessly. "Well, anyone but myself."

"Then I'll have to make this worth the wait," he said, settling over her, making a place for himself between her thighs.

"It already has been. It was worth the wait the first time you kissed me."

"Where do you keep your condoms?" he asked.

Wait, *what?* "Where do *I* keep them? That is a joke, right?"

"Do I look as if I'm joking?"

No, he didn't. "Colin, here in the U.S., that's typically the man's responsibility."

Looking thoroughly confused, he said, "Well, where I'm from, the woman supplies the contraceptives."

"Seriously?"

A grin tilted the corners of his mouth. "No, not really."

He reached over to his pants and pulled a chain of half a dozen out of the pocket.

"That was so not funny," she said.

He laughed. "Yes, it was. You should have seen your face."

If she hadn't been so relieved, she probably would have socked him one. She did the next best thing. She shoved him over onto his back and straddled his thighs. "You know I'm going to have to get you back for that. And it will be when you least expect it."

If he was worried, it didn't show.

"Come here," he said, pulling her down so he could kiss her. Then the earth tilted, and suddenly she was on her back again, Colin's weight pushing her into the blanket. When she tried to shove him back over, he grabbed her wrists and pinned her arms over her head.

"Where do you think you're going?"

He clearly preferred to be the one in control. The problem with that was, so did she.

"I like to be on top," she said, pushing against his hands.

"And I like to dominate," he said, refusing to let go.

With each of them volleying for the upper hand, it turned into an all-out wrestling match. With the occasional illegal move—a pinch here, a bite there. And since neither would surrender the high ground, they finally compromised and did it standing up in the kitchen, her back pressed against the cool refrigerator door, her legs wrapped around Colin's hips as he thrust into her, cheesy, decade-old refrigerator magnets dropping on the faded linoleum floor. And though he was doing just fine without her help, and she was more or less holding on for the ride, she couldn't resist panting an occasional suggestion or two. "Kiss me here" or "touch me there" and a random "faster" or "harder." Until she was so mindless from the pleasure, her brain ceased to function and her baser instincts took over. And this time, when she shattered, he was right there with her.

"Wow," Colin said, dropping his head on her shoulder, breathing hard. "Are you always so bossy?"

"Bossy? *Me?*"

He lifted his head and pinned her with a *yeah, right* look.

She opened her mouth to argue, then reconsidered. "I guess I am."

"Have I ever mentioned that I like a woman who knows what she wants?"

Lucky her. "So I was wondering if we might be able to do that again."

Looking amused, he said, "Were you under the impression that we were done?"

"I wasn't sure. I mean, I hoped we weren't."

"We're just getting started," he said with a sexy grin. "And this time, I might even let you be on top."

The next night, while Rowena was waiting for Betty, her phone rang, and the number that popped up on the caller ID belonged to Cara. Rowena had forgotten all about their Angelica Pierce conversation.

Rowena assumed she had some sort of information, but

instead Cara told her, "Block out the last week in March on your calendar. You're coming to D.C."

"I am?"

"Well, I figured you wouldn't want to miss my *wedding!*"

"You and Max set a date! Congratulations! And of *course* I want to be there."

Cara laughed. "Like I thought you would say no. It's probably going to be a small ceremony, but feel free to bring a date. In fact, I'm hoping you do."

Rowena's first thought was Colin, of course. As if that would ever happen. They'd had their one night, and now it was over. And despite what he said, he never really had let her get on top. Something she would always regret missing.

"I actually have someone in mind," Rowena told her.

"You do?" Cara said, sounding excited. "Who?"

"Well, he's really cute. He has naturally curly red hair, hazel eyes, about thirty inches tall…"

Cara laughed. "I was thinking someone just a bit older, but we would love it if you brought Dylan. Oh, and by the way, I did put out the feelers on Angelica, but with every thing that's been going on, I haven't had time to follow up."

"To be honest, I haven't even thought about it, so don't feel rushed. I've been so busy lately I haven't been keeping up with the news."

"Well, Ariella has been so bombarded by the media that she went back into hiding, and Eleanor Albert seems to have fallen off the face of the earth. No one knows where she disappeared to."

Rowena felt so bad for Ariella. She didn't know her well, but the few times they had crossed paths, she seemed very nice.

Rowena and Caroline talked for a few minutes more, until Betty came in.

"I'm assuming this is for you," Betty said, handing her a letter-sized white envelope. "It was taped to your door."

Curious, Rowena tore it open. Inside was a folded sheet of white paper with two words penned in unfamiliar handwriting.

Pool House.

Hadn't they decided that last night was going to be their one and only time together? That it wasn't worth getting caught?

She walked to the pool house, rehearsing in her head how she would turn him down.

The pool house was dark, but the door was unlocked. She opened it and stepped inside. There was a lit candle on the coffee table, the blanket was spread out on the floor and Colin, dressed in a pair of faded jeans and nothing else, sat in the middle of it. She opened her mouth to speak, only to find that her carefully rehearsed excuses were forgotten.

"I had dinner with your father tonight," he said.

"Oh. That's…nice."

"He actually wasn't feeling well. Migraine, he said. So he took a sleeping pill and went to bed. I don't imagine there's any chance of him waking up and coming down to the pool."

No, when he took a sleeping pill he was usually down for the night.

"We said one time," she reminded him, but her legs were already carrying her across the room to the blanket.

"You're right, we did. So, what's to stop us from saying one *more* time?"

"The more chances we take, the more likely we are to get caught."

"That's what makes it so much fun." He flashed her that sizzling grin, and she was done for.

"Okay, but this is the absolute last time," she said, tugging her cover-up over her head. "And only on one condition."

"Name it," he said, watching as she peeled her bathing suit off and made herself comfortable straddling his thighs.

"This time," she said, "*I* get to be on top."

Eight

Two nights turned into three, and three into four, until Rowena and Colin finally admitted that they were having themselves a full-blown affair. One that they agreed would end when he went back to England. That was the part Colin was feeling slightly ambivalent about.

Not that he was thinking marriage, or even long term. The truth was, he didn't know what he was feeling. Maybe because she was a complete departure from the spoiled and pampered socialites he'd dated in the past. The ones who accepted his decision to keep things casual, then did whatever they could to snag their claws in. Rowena didn't have claws, or inhibitions, and she certainly knew how to have fun. And though she had made her share of mistakes, they had clearly given her an interesting outlook on life. She was sexy and intelligent and fun. And tough. She spoke her mind, even if what she said wasn't popular opinion. He found himself fascinated by nearly everything that came out of her mouth. At the same time, she knew when it was better to say nothing at all.

Unless he flat-out asked about Dylan, she didn't bring him up, and when he did ask, her answers were brief and very vague. As if her affair with Colin and her relationship with her son were two things that she wouldn't mix. He wasn't sure if she did it to keep a safe distance between Dylan and Colin, or Colin and herself.

Whatever the reason, he didn't waste too much time worrying about it, especially now that they had just been handed a free pass for the entire weekend. Her father was flying to Washington in the morning for some critical senatorial vote, and, expecting a filibuster from the opposing side of the aisle, he wouldn't be coming back until Tuesday evening.

Colin was hoping he could talk her into spending those evenings in her suite. Or his. The pool house served its purpose, but the hard floor, where they were currently lying side by side, naked and sated, was getting old fast.

"What am I going to tell Betty?" Rowena asked him. "She watches Dylan every night."

"Tell her you have swimmer's elbow and you need a few days off."

She looked over at him and laughed. "Swimmer's elbow?"

"Or here's a thought. You could come to my suite for an hour and a half. Then when Betty leaves, I'll come to you. As long as I'm gone before the staff is up, we should be good, right?"

"Are you saying that you want to sleep over?"

"Who said anything about sleeping?"

He thought women liked having men sleep over. He'd certainly been asked to enough. Rowena looked as if she wasn't sure what to think.

"What I don't understand is why my father would be so adamant about you not pursuing me," she said. "He's always wanted me to marry an independently wealthy man with a good bloodline and political contacts. You've got it all, *plus* a royal title. You're like his dream son-in-law."

"I can think of one good reason. He thinks I'm a womanizer."

"Are you?"

He made a *pfft* sound. "Certainly not."

"Are you sure?"

"Of course I'm sure." The word had such a negative connotation. He was a gentleman. He treated women with respect.

"To be honest, I'm not even sure the exact definition."

Since he wasn't one, he had never experienced any burning need to know.

"Just for fun…" She held up her phone. "Let's look it up."

She tapped away at the screen for a minute, then said, "Here it is. According to my phone dictionary, a womanizer is 'a man who engages in numerous casual sexual affairs with women.'" She looked over at him. "Do you do that?"

"That can't be right," he said.

She pointed to her phone. "It says it right here."

He sat up and held out his hand. "Let me see that."

He took it and read the definition on the screen. "I'll be damned."

She nodded sympathetically, holding her hand out for her phone. "The truth hurts, huh?"

"I would hardly say that I'm sexually promiscuous. I love women. I *respect* them."

She shrugged. "Just lots of different ones."

He glared at her. "I have never slept with a woman

without first making it clear that it will never be anything but casual."

"And you think that makes it okay?"

"I'm a gentleman. I pamper women."

"You mean you *buy* them."

She was twisting his words. "That isn't what I said."

"What makes you think you're so special?"

Now she was putting words in his mouth. "I don't recall saying I was special."

"Let's do this. Take the same situation, but take out the man and put a woman in instead. She dates often, sleeps with different men, pampers them and only wants to keep it casual. What does that make her?"

"The perfect woman?"

It was her turn to glare at him. "It makes her a slut, Colin. So why should the exact behavior be perfectly acceptable for a man?"

He hated to admit it, but she was right. So, by definition, he *was* a womanizer. "I suppose that I am in fact a slut."

"Welcome to the club. We've got jackets."

He shook his head and laughed.

"Hey, I have a *great* idea," she said. "If we do get caught, we can just tell my father that it's my fault. I came on to you, and though you tried to resist, I wouldn't leave you alone, so you finally gave in and let me have my way with you."

"You do have some dominance issues." Not that he was complaining. It definitely kept things interesting. He was sure that any day now she was going to whip out the handcuffs or silk scarves.

"It's not as if he could have a lower opinion of me. I had a child out of wedlock. In his mind, that labels me a slut for life."

"I doubt he thinks that. He's just protecting you."

"This has nothing to do with him protecting me. The only person he's protecting is himself. He doesn't want you around me because he thinks that I'm the same mixed-up heathen I was before I had Dylan. He thinks I'll embarrass him or, even worse, corrupt you and drag you down to my level."

"That's ridiculous. I can take care of myself."

"Try to tell him that." She pushed herself up and grabbed her bathing suit.

"Where are you going?"

"It's getting late," she said, tugging the suit on.

He picked up her phone to check the time. "We still have twenty minutes."

"Colin, you take *way* longer than twenty minutes."

"So let's just talk."

"I'm tired." She pulled on her cover-up, then leaned down and kissed him. Not the slow, lingering kind. Just a quick peck. "Besides, we have all weekend, right?"

He got up, wrapped a blanket around his waist and followed her to the door. "Did I say something that upset you?"

"Of course not," she said, but her smile didn't quite reach her eyes. "Call me at work tomorrow and we'll decide what we want to do."

"You're sure everything is okay?"

"Everything is great," she said, but as he watched her walk away, he didn't believe her.

What was Colin's deal? Why was he getting so…touchy-feely? So personal? It was supposed to be just sex, and now he wanted to *talk?* Where had *that* come from?

Lately it seemed Rowena was spending an awful lot of time convincing herself that Colin was not as wonderful as her brain was trying to make her believe. She would only wind up hurt. He was too good for her, and if he didn't realize that, if he was actually having feelings for her, someone needed to clue him in.

When she got back to her room, Betty was watching television.

"Good swim?" Betty asked.

"Oh, yes, very refreshing." *Not.* "How was Dylan?"

"Didn't make a peep."

Betty usually left the minute Rowena got there, but this time she didn't even get off the couch. Exhausted, both physically and mentally, Rowena flopped down beside her and laid her head on her shoulder, inhaling the familiar scent of her gardenia perfume. The same scent she'd worn as long as Rowena could remember.

"You know what I find remarkable?" Betty said.

"Hmm?"

"That for the last four days, you've managed to swim ninety minutes' worth of laps without getting your hair wet. You don't even smell like chlorine."

Rowena's breath backed up in her lungs. *Oh, crap.* Rowena was an intelligent woman. Had it not even occurred to her to take a quick dive into the pool before coming inside?

"Don't beat yourself up over it," Betty said, patting her knee. "You've been so happy lately I would have known something was up anyway."

She sat up. "I've been happy?"

"More than I've seen you in years."

"Even after Dylan?"

"That was a different kind of happy. Lately, you've been glowing. That new-love glow."

"Betty, if my dad finds out—"

"Sweetheart, he isn't going to hear it from me, and as far as the rest of the staff are concerned, there are more who have drifted over to your camp in the last year or two than you would probably believe. If I hear anyone breathe a word about it, I'll set them straight."

Well, that was nice to know. Not everyone thought she was a complete screwup. "Thank you. And as for the glowing thing, love has nothing to do with it. We're keeping it casual."

"If you say so."

"I do."

"Would it be so terrible to let yourself feel happy?"

It wasn't that simple. Happiness always came with a price, and it just wasn't worth the pain and disappointment of having to let it go.

After watching the senator's limo drive away the next morning, Colin walked down the path to the day care with the box of books his sister had mailed to him. Children's books he intended to donate to the day care. It was an excellent excuse to see Rowena. He couldn't shake the feeling that something had been bothering her last night, and he wanted to know what.

He hit the buzzer at the gate, and a few seconds later Tricia appeared.

"Good morning, Colin." She opened the gate and let him on the playground. He spotted Dylan, digging in the sandbox with a little girl who looked to be close to his age, but no Rowena.

"Is Rowena in her office?" he asked Tricia.

"She's home sick today. Caught the flu. It's nearly impossible to avoid in this line of work. I swear I spend ninety percent of my life fighting the sniffles."

"Cowin!"

Colin turned to see Dylan hobbling over excitedly, faster than a walk, but not quite a run. Despite all the kid had been through in his short life, he sure seemed happy all the time.

"Hey, bud," Colin said, surprised when Dylan threw himself at his legs, hugging them hard. For a kid so frail-looking, he had one hell of a grip.

He gazed up at Colin, frowned and said, "Mommy sick."

"I know. Do you think I should go back to the mansion and check on her?"

Dylan's eyes lit up. "Me, too! Me, too!"

"No way, kiddo," Tricia said. "You know your mommy wants you to stay down here with me."

His lower lip curled into a pout and Tricia pried him from Colin's legs, scooping him up onto her hip. Then she grinned at Colin and said, "I'll bet, if you ask nice, Colin would give Mommy a kiss for you."

"Kiss Mommy! Kiss Mommy!"

"But don't girls have cooties?" Colin asked.

Dylan giggled. "Not *mommies*."

The little girl Dylan had been playing with called his name, so he wiggled out of Tricia's arms and hobbled back to the sandbox.

"It's a little late in the game to be worrying about cooties, don't you think?" Tricia said. "What with all the swimming you two have been doing. But don't worry, my lips are sealed. This is the happiest I've seen her in a really long time."

And he was happy to be the person making her happy.

"I brought these for the day care," he said, handing Tricia the box. "It's just some old books I thought the children might like."

"Thank you, Colin!" She looked at the address on the label. "You ordered them all the way from England?"

"Actually these are the books I had when I was a boy."

"That's so nice of you to do. Are you sure you don't want to save them for when you have kids?"

"I'm sure." He didn't know if he would ever have children of his own. That would require settling down, and he wasn't sure if he wanted to do that. He had a friend from the army who had started his own private security firm, and he wanted Colin to come work for him. He hadn't given him an answer yet, but now that he was nearly recuperated, he had to give some serious thought as to what he planned to do next.

"Well, I should go," he said, walking to the gate. "Enjoy the books."

"Hey, Colin?" Tricia said.

He turned back to her.

"Rowena seems tough, but she's actually very vulnerable."

He'd figured that out pretty early in the game. "I know that."

"I've never seen her so happy, but this is also a very difficult time for her. If you take advantage of her, or hurt her, royal or not, I will hunt you down and make you pay."

He didn't bother to point out that two people rarely went into a relationship of any kind expecting to hurt each other, yet it did happen from time to time.

He walked back up to the mansion, running into Betty on his way past the kitchen.

"I don't suppose you're on your way upstairs," she said.

"I am, actually."

"Could you do me a favor? I don't know if you heard, but Rowena isn't feeling well. Could you stop by her suite and give her these?" She dropped a stack of clean linens and blankets in his arms. "With the rain coming my arthritis is bad, especially going up and down all those stairs. Would you mind?"

"No, not at all. As long as you don't think she'll mind."

"I think we both know the answer to that," Betty said, giving him a wink.

"Did Rowena tell you...?"

She smiled and patted his arm. "She didn't have to."

And by sending Colin up with the linens, she'd given him the perfect excuse to see her.

"Thanks, Betty."

She just smiled. "If she needs anything, you tell her to call down."

Colin walked upstairs and knocked on the door to Rowena's suite. He heard an incoherent mumble from the other side and, assuming it was an invitation, he let himself in. The television was on and Rowena was curled up in a ball on the couch, an afghan tucked tightly around her, eyes closed, looking pale and listless.

"Caught a bug, have we?" he said.

Her eyes fluttered open, and when she saw that it was him standing there, she gasped and pulled the covers over her head, mumbling from underneath, "What are you doing here?"

"Tricia told me you were sick, and Betty sent me up to give you these blankets and linens. How are you feeling?"

"Like death, and I'm sure I look like it, too. I haven't even brushed my hair."

"Have you called a physician?"

She peeked her head out from under the afghan. "It's this god-awful flu that's going around. I'll be fine in a day or two. And you shouldn't even be here. Trust me when I say you do not want to catch this."

Instead of backing off, he sat on the edge of the couch cushion right beside her. "Considering all the time we've spent together, odds are good I've already caught it. Have you taken your temperature?"

She shook her head.

"What are your symptoms?"

"Fever, chills, body aches and I think my head might explode. But the ibuprofen is helping."

He sat on the edge of the cushion and held his wrist to Rowena's forehead, the way his sister had done when Colin was sick as a boy. She felt a little warm, but not enough to cause concern. "Is there anything I can get you?"

"You don't have to take care of me. Betty checks on me every so often, and I can call her if I need anything."

"Have you had water?"

"Some, when I got up this morning."

"You should be drinking fluids to stay hydrated. Have you eaten anything?"

She shook her head. "Not since dinner last night."

"When I was young, and I had the flu, my sister Matilda fixed me chicken soup." He paused and added, "Well, she had the maid fix it for me. But she always sat with me while I ate it, and read me stories until I fell asleep."

"Why your sister and not your parents?"

"Matty is twenty years older than me, and when I wasn't off at boarding school, she raised me."

"Why her?"

"I was born quite late in my parents' lives. My father was sixty, my mother forty-seven. I was unplanned, and neither seemed to have much interest in starting over, especially with a demanding and precocious little boy like myself."

"Demanding and precocious? I'd never have guessed."

"I had a fondness for setting things on fire."

Her runny, bloodshot eyes went wide. "Seriously?"

He looked around the room, then said, "You have good insurance, yes?"

Her smile was weak, but genuine.

"The truth is, my days as an arsonist ended when I set fire to the boys' loo at boarding school. Suffice it to say, the punishment more than fit the crime."

"Sounds like it was a cry for attention."

"I imagine it was."

"Does your sister have a family of her own?"

"No. She married young, before I was born, but her husband became ill shortly after and died. She was pregnant—which I gather is why they married in the first place—but she lost the baby. She never remarried or had other children."

"That's so sad."

"I used to pretend that my parents were actually my grandparents, and Matty was really my mum. She loved me as if she were. To this day she still tries to baby me."

"Could it be possible that she is?"

He laughed and shook his head. "No, no chance. It was just a dejected child's foolish fantasy."

"Are your parents still living?"

"My father passed away when I was at university. My mother is still alive and staying with my sister, but she's not doing well."

"Do you see her often?"

"Once or twice a year."

"That's it?"

"Matty implores me to visit more, but there's no real… emotional attachment."

"I wish I only had to see my father once a year." She paused, looking distraught, and said, "Oh, no, this was supposed to be our weekend. I'm ruining it."

"There will be other weekends. Or you might feel fine by tomorrow. We'll just wait and see."

"Okay."

"Would you be more comfortable in bed?"

"Probably, but Dylan spilled juice all over my sheets and blankets this morning when he was trying to bring me breakfast."

"Why don't I change them for you, so you can lie down?"

"Colin, you don't have to do that."

"I know I don't. I want to." He grabbed the sheets and blankets and carried them to her bedroom. What looked like dried grape juice was splattered across the sheets and duvet, and there were spots on the carpet, as well. He stripped the bed, inhaling the scent of her skin. She was so familiar to him now. He knew how she smelled, how she tasted, every curve of her body. He knew just where to touch her to bring her off, or how to take his time and drive her slowly out of her mind until she was begging for release. He liked that above all else sex with her was not only extremely satisfying, but fun. She didn't expect to be treated like a princess or require sappy sentiments of affection. She didn't talk about making love. They had sex, plain and simple, and they did it very well.

He fixed the bed, then helped her up from the couch. She was so woozy she teetered a bit. He led her to her room and helped her into bed. "Now, let's see if I remember how to do this."

Confused, she asked, "Do what?"

"Tuck you in. If I recall, first you lie down. Which you have done. Then covers, right?" He pulled the covers up all the way to her chin, then tucked them firmly around her shoulders. "Are you warm enough?"

She nodded.

"I feel as if I'm forgetting something."

"I don't think so," she said.

"Oh, I remember…" He leaned down and pressed a kiss

to her forehead. "I have some work to do, but I'll knock you up in an hour or two."

She blinked. "I'm sorry, you'll do what?"

"Knock you up, knock on your door."

"Oh, okay, good. For a minute there I though you meant something totally different."

He kissed her forehead again and said, "See you in a bit."

"Colin, you don't have to."

No, but oddly enough, he *wanted* to.

Nine

Rowena tossed and turned for a while, then settled into a deep dreamless sleep. She woke later, disoriented by the fact that it was light out, since she usually woke at the crack of dawn. Without her contacts in, she couldn't see the clock. But when she moved, and her achy muscles screamed in protest, she remembered that she was sick.

Colin must have anticipated her condition, because there were ibuprofen pills and a glass of ice water on the bedside table.

She sat up to take the pills, thinking she might be well enough for a shower, but she was so woozy, and her body so sore and limp, she wasn't sure she would even make it to the bathroom. She closed her eyes and must have fallen right back to sleep, because when she opened them again the room was dark.

What time was it? And who was taking care of Dylan?

She shot up in bed, still feeling weak and dizzy. "Colin?" she called. "Betty? *Anybody?*"

Colin appeared in the doorway an instant later. "You're awake."

"How long did I sleep? Is it really dark out?"

"It's nine-thirty." He switched on the lamp and she squinted as the light burned her retinas.

"At *night?*" She couldn't recall ever having slept this long in her adult life, and she couldn't say she felt any better for it. She felt so lousy, in fact, she didn't even care how dreadful she must have looked. "Where is Dylan? I have to make him dinner."

"Dylan and I had dinner hours ago. He's in bed."

"You had dinner *together?*"

"Betty's chicken pot pie. That woman is a genius in the kitchen."

"I should go check on him," she said, but when she tried to move, she could barely get up on her elbows. It felt as if someone had covered her with a lead blanket.

"Relax," Colin said. "I've been checking on him every fifteen minutes. He's fine."

"He has medication to take—"

"Betty showed me the list. He's all set for the night."

"Betty knows you're here?"

"I get the feeling she knows everything. I assume you've talked to her about us."

"We talked. She won't rat us out."

Unable to hold herself up another instant, she dropped back against the mattress. "I'm so sorry you had to do this."

"Don't be. We had fun. Dylan is a great kid."

A great kid who didn't need to get attached to a man, then have him walk away.

"Are you hungry?" Colin asked.

She shook her head. Her symptoms this morning didn't even compare to how wretched she felt now. Everything ached, as if someone had worked her over from head to toe, but from the inside. Though she knew it was physically impossible, even her hair throbbed.

"I think maybe I need more ibuprofen," she said. Or a gun.

She was so weak and jittery Colin had to help her sit up, and he held the water glass while she took the pills. Then he set the glass on the bedside table.

"Could you have Betty come up here so I can ask her to stay over? If Dylan wakes in the middle of the night and I'm this sick, I won't be able to take care of him."

"She offered to stay, but I told her she didn't have to."

"Why?"

"Because I'm staying here tonight."

"Colin, you really don't have to do that."

"You're right, I don't. But I want to."

But why? Why would he take a chance getting caught? And why was he hanging around, taking care of her? Taking care of her son? This was supposed to be an affair. Just sex. She was already starting to really like him, and he was only making it worse.

"Why don't you get back to sleep?" he said, pressing a kiss to her forehead. "You'll feel better tomorrow."

She hoped so. She couldn't imagine feeling any worse. And before she could lodge another protest, he was gone. She was so weak, following him wasn't even an option. So she fell right back to sleep instead. She roused once in the middle of the night and could swear she saw the outline of a body lying in bed next to her, and though she meant to reach over and feel the mattress, she must have fallen back to sleep before she had the chance. When she woke up again the room was bright. She heard morning sounds coming from the kitchen and Dylan's infectious giggle. Had Colin really been in bed with her, or had it been some

fever-induced, vivid dream? The covers were so dishev-
eled from all of her tossing and turning, it was hard to say.

She pushed herself up into a sitting position, relieved to
discover that although she still felt weak, nothing seemed
to be hurting today. Not even her head. Her tummy rum-
bled and the aroma of fresh coffee coaxed her out of bed,
but when she saw her reflection in the bathroom mirror,
she gasped. Her hair was so matted it looked dreadlocked.
No way she wanted Colin to see her looking this bad.

Shower, *then* coffee.

Colin got Dylan dressed, fed and medicated, then settled in front of the television watching Saturday-morning
kids' shows. For a two-and-a-half-year-old special-needs
child, Dylan was independent and extremely capable—
or so it seemed to Colin—and pretty darned easy to care
for. He had expected Dylan to be upset that his mother
wasn't around, but he seemed to understand that she was
sick and needed rest. Maybe because it was something
with which he had personal experience. Too much personal experience.

When Colin had rolled out of bed an hour ago, Rowena was sleeping peacefully, but when he stepped into
her room to check on her now, the bed was empty and he
could hear the shower running in the bathroom. He hoped
that meant she was feeling better today. She had been so
out of it yesterday that he'd begun to worry about her, and
if she hadn't improved by this morning he was going to
insist she see a doctor. The fact that she had the energy to
make it to the shower unaided was a good sign.

"Cowin!" Dylan called from the living room. When
Colin stepped into the room, Dylan held out his cup—or
sippy, as he called it—and said, "Duce peez?" Which Colin
had learned meant *juice please*. He was getting quite adept

at translating Dylan's speech. There were still questionable words, but usually he could figure out what the boy meant.

"Apple juice?" Colin said.

Dylan smiled and nodded vigorously.

Colin got his juice, then put the breakfast dishes in the dishwasher and wiped down the counters. He had just finished when Rowena emerged from her bedroom. She was dressed in flannel pajama bottoms and a Lakers sweatshirt, she wore no makeup and her hair was wet, but she looked to be on the way to recovery.

"Good morning," he said. "Feeling better today, I see."

"Still a little weak, but I feel human again."

Dylan heard her voice and screeched, "Mommy!"

She smiled. "Hey, honey."

He got up from the rug where he'd been sitting and hobbled over to Rowena. Colin had realized that although Dylan looked unsteady on his feet, he actually had fairly good balance, all things considered, and maybe if Rowena let him spread his wings a little, he would walk even better.

Rowena picked him up and gave him a big hug. Dylan launched into a long explanation of everything he and Colin had done while she was sick, everything they had eaten, what books they had read before bed last night. The kid didn't miss a thing. And though some of it was still a little hard to understand, the last thing he said was crystal clear. When Rowena said, "It sounds like you had fun with Colin," Dylan nodded and said, "He be my daddy?"

Whoa. His *daddy?*

Colin hadn't been expecting that, and clearly neither had Rowena. Stunned, she looked over to Colin, then back to Dylan as if she didn't know what to say. But one thing

Colin had learned was that toddlers—even ones as smart as Dylan—were easily distracted.

"Hey, Dylan, did you want to show Mummy what you made her in art class yesterday?"

Dylan's face lit up and he shifted to get out of her arms. "I geddit!"

She put him down and he scurried off to his room, not exactly running, but moving pretty fast.

"I'm so sorry about that," she told Colin, looking utterly horrified.

"It's okay."

"I have absolutely no idea where that came from. He's never done it before with anyone."

"Rowena—"

"He gets confused. His friends talk about their daddies and…of course I don't date, so his exposure to men is limited. Not that I think we're *dating*."

He touched her arm. "It's okay. You don't have to explain. I guess it never occurred to me that my being around would confuse Dylan. If I had known I wouldn't have insisted on staying. I'm sorry if I put you in a difficult situation."

"It seems lately there are so many things he wants, so much I want to give him but can't. I feel as if I'm failing him."

Dylan hobbled back into the room to give his mommy the picture he'd made at day care yesterday.

"Oh, baby, I love it!" Colin heard her say as he walked into the kitchen, and he could swear there were tears in her voice. How could she possibly think she was failing Dylan? He was happy and smart and as healthy as he could be—and according to Betty, mostly due to Rowena's diligence. And Dylan clearly loved her to death. If there was anything he wanted but didn't have, Colin was sure it was for a good reason, and not her fault in the least. From behind him Rowena asked, "Hey, any chance I could score a cup of that coffee?"

Rowena could hardly believe that after Dylan's daddy comment, Colin hadn't made a beeline for the door. But there he was, still in her kitchen.

"How about something to eat?" he asked her. "You must be famished."

"I am pretty hungry, but I could just have cereal."

"Nonsense." He opened the refrigerator and pulled out the plate of leftover pancakes. "I saved you these."

"Oh! Betty's famous flapjacks?"

"Not quite." At her confused look, he said, "I made them."

"Oh. Yeah, sure. I'll have some."

Colin laughed. "Don't worry, they're edible."

"I didn't even realize I had pancake mix."

"You didn't. I made them from scratch."

Really?

He slid the plate into the microwave, set the time and pressed the start button, then poured her coffee. "Cream? Sugar?"

"Black." He handed her the cup and she took a sip, sighing with pleasure. There was nothing like a good, strong cup of coffee to start the day. "I didn't know you could cook."

"There are a lot of things you don't know about me."

Was it her imagination, or did he sound almost as if he thought that was a bad thing?

They were having an affair. Sex only. No meaningful conversations required.

The microwave dinged and Colin set the plate in front

of her. She slathered the pancakes in butter and syrup, then took a bite. "Oh, my God! These are delicious!"

She scarfed them down, and getting some food in her stomach made a world of difference.

"So I'm thinking it would be best, so as not to confuse Dylan, if we only saw each other when he isn't around," Colin said.

"I think that would be best. We have a week and a half. This is supposed to be about having fun. Let's not complicate it with personal stuff."

God knows her life would be complicated enough in the coming months. In her free time she had been finalizing her plans, and if all went well, and stayed on schedule, she would be putting that plan into action soon.

"I'm going to go take care of a few things," Colin said. "Why don't you text me later, after Dylan is in bed. Betty mentioned that most of the staff is gone on the weekends, so if we're careful, getting caught shouldn't be a concern."

Betty was so awesome, and Rowena loved her for it. "I'll do that."

"You know, last night I finally got you into a real bed, and all we did was sleep."

So that *was* him.

"I'll see you later," Colin said. He looked over at Dylan, who was mesmerized by the television, then pressed a quick kiss to her lips. "Text me."

When he was gone, Rowena sat down in one of the kitchen chairs to drink her coffee. She was relieved to have some time to herself, what with all of the things she still had to do, though she was limited on the weekends since every government agency she would need to contact was closed.

She was on her second cup of coffee when Cara called.

"It's official," she told Rowena. "I've hit a dead end.

I've searched the internet and asked around, and no one seems to know what happened to Madeline. It's as if she vanished into thin air."

"Or changed her name to Angelica Pierce and had a serious makeover. You wouldn't happen to have a yearbook from high school from before the time she was expelled."

"Somewhere. Do you?"

"I think it may be in storage with my other stuff in D.C., but I'm not sure when I'll have a chance to look for it." She wasn't planning a trip to Washington anytime soon. Like in this century.

"I'll see if I can find mine, then."

"By the way, have you talked to Ariella?"

"Yeah. She's still in shock, I think."

Who wouldn't be if they learned they might be the president's illegitimate child? "Has she met with him yet?"

"Not yet. She said they're going to wait for the DNA test results to come in. Until then she's lying low."

"Has anyone heard from the alleged birth mom?"

"Eleanor Albert is in the wind, as they say."

"Well, send my best to Ariella and tell her I'm keeping her in my thoughts."

"She'll appreciate that. She's such a sweet person. She doesn't deserve this."

They talked for several minutes about the latest D.C. gossip—who was sleeping with or bribing whom, and other juicy tidbits, then they hung up so Rowena could get herself and Dylan ready to go.

Dylan was still mesmerized by the television. Rowena tried to limit his TV time to two hours a day, and only educational programming. But on the weekends she made exceptions. Especially if she had things to do that were difficult to accomplish with a toddler vying for her attention. Although right now Rowena was the one feeling distracted.

She finally closed her laptop and called to Dylan, "Hey, pumpkin, you want to go to the playground for a while?"

Dylan's head snapped in her direction, and his eyes lit up. "Cowin come, too!"

Damn. They needed to have a talk about this. She walked over and sat on the rug beside him. "No, Dylan, Colin is not coming with us. He only stayed here because mommy was sick and he wanted to help. Like when you have to go to the hospital and the nurses and doctors all help each other take care of you. Just like when you hit your head and Colin fixed your boo-boo."

Dylan nodded, then said, "He be my daddy?"

She sighed. The message just wasn't getting through. "No, sweetheart, he's not going to be your daddy. But he can be your friend."

"I don't have a daddy," he said, so matter-of-factly it broke her heart.

"Some kids don't have daddies, but that only means that their mommies love them extra, extra special," she said, tickling his ribs until he was out of breath from giggling. "Now go get your shoes and your backpack. And you can bring *one* toy."

"Yeah!"

She watched him hobble down the hall to his room, so sweet and innocent, her heart bursting with love for him. And out of nowhere she had the inexplicable feeling that despite everything he had been through, and everything he had to face in the future, he would be okay. He would succeed and be happy.

She only wished she felt so hopeful about her own life.

Ten

Rowena and Dylan played on the playground until lunch-time, then as a special treat she took him to his favorite fast-food restaurant. She even let him have a caffeine-free soda. In the not-so-distant future there wouldn't be money for these little luxuries. She would be counting her pennies.

She tucked Dylan in at seven-thirty and he was asleep before his head hit the pillow.

She thought tonight it would be nice to do something a little different, so she stripped out of her clothes and changed into the lace teddy that was a hold-over from before she had Dylan. It was snug, but it fit. She pulled her silk robe on and belted it at the waist, then brushed her hair out and dabbed on lipstick. Usually when Colin and she met at the pool house they were so anxious to get naked and get to the good stuff, she didn't bother with sexy clothes or makeup. For them, the seduction phase was obsolete. Intercourse was a forgone conclusion. To-night would be a little different. They would have almost all night, and she couldn't deny that she was looking forward to having sex in a real bed for a change.

Instead of typing out a text, she opened the robe and took a photo of herself and texted that instead. And he must have been ready to go, because he was knocking on her door a minute or two later.

She opened it, and he made a growly noise in his throat when he saw her.

"Is this for me?" he asked, slipping inside, reaching out to run his fingers over the lace covering her belly.

"I thought it would be a nice change of pace."

"I'd have come here in my silk pajamas, but not only would it be difficult to explain if someone were to see me, but I don't actually own silk pajamas."

"I like what you're wearing now." The jogging pants were very easy access, and the nylon muscle shirt showed off his extraordinary pecs. How could she be so lucky that her first time back in the ring was with someone so unbelievably hot and awesome in bed…or on the floor, as was typically the case.

"Out of curiosity, what do you wear to sleep?" she asked.

"Nothing."

Oh, well, that would be nice, too. "We have most of the night, so there's no need to rush things. Would you like to start off with something to drink? I have iced tea and soda, or I could sneak down to the den and nab you a bottle of scotch."

"I think I'd just like water," he said, pinching the bridge of his nose with his thumb and forefinger.

"You all right?" she asked.

"Fine. I'm just a little tired. It was a busy week."

It certainly had been. "Have a seat. I'll get the water."

She filled two of her nicer drink glasses with ice and

filtered water, feeling a tiny bit nervous. Not about the sex—because they had no problems in that department—but because he was going to be there awhile. When they weren't having sex, what would they talk about? What would they do? What if, when the sex was over, they got bored with each other?

Worst case, she could always pretend to fall asleep.

She walked back into the living room and set their drinks on the coffee table. Colin sat on the sofa, his head back against the cushion and lolled to one side, his eyes closed.

She sat beside him and touched his arm. "Wake up, sleepyhead."

He blinked awake. "I'm sorry, did I drift off?"

"I guess so."

He yawned. "I'm knackered."

"Which means?"

"Exhausted." He reached up and rubbed his left temple, wincing. "And I've got an awful headache."

She folded her arms. "Isn't that supposed to be my excuse?"

"It's no excuse. I'm honestly not feeling well."

He did look a little pale and his eyes were bloodshot. She pressed her wrist to his forehead. "Colin, you have a fever."

"Bloody hell," he muttered. "I suppose I should have anticipated this."

"Let's go," she said, offering a hand to give him a boost. "You'll be more comfortable in bed."

He sighed and let his head fall back against the cushions. "Could you give me a minute before you kick me out?"

Kick him out? "I meant *my* bed, Colin."

His brows rose in surprise.

"After all you did for me, did you honestly think I wouldn't take care of you?"

"I don't want to be a burden."

She rolled her eyes. "Please, save me the tough-guy spiel. Like it or not, you're stuck with me until you're well. Now get up."

"What about Dylan?"

"I'll just keep the bedroom door closed and locked in the morning before we go down to the day care. He'll never even know you were here."

"And the staff?"

"If anyone asks, I'll tell Betty to say that you're in your suite, not feeling well, and don't want to be disturbed. And if your flu is anything like mine was, you'll be back to your old self by Tuesday when the senator is due home. Now let's go."

He took her hand and let her pull him up.

"You know, I really would be fine on my own," he said as she led him to the bedroom.

"Uh-huh. Sure you would." Men were notoriously big babies when they were sick. Of course, being a soldier, maybe he was tougher than the average guy.

She switched on the bedroom light and pulled back the covers on the bed. "I changed the sheets this morning, so they're fresh. Is there anything you need from your suite? Pajamas maybe?"

He shook his head and looked longingly at the bed, as if he couldn't wait to lie down.

"Go ahead and climb in and I'll get you some ibuprofen."

She got his ice water from the coffee table and grabbed the pill bottle. Colin sat on the edge of the bed, dressed in nothing but black boxer briefs, looking like a freaking underwear ad.

"We get a weekend together, and this happens," he said.

"Maybe you'll feel better tomorrow night." She tapped two tablets into her hand and gave them to him.

He swallowed them, then stretched out, so tall that his feet nearly hung off the bottom edge of the bed. She pulled the covers up over him, then sat beside him and checked his forehead again. He was really hot.

"Have I mentioned that I think you're an excellent mum?"

She smiled. "I have my moments, I guess."

"Take it from someone whose mum didn't have a bloody clue. Dylan is lucky to have you."

"Mine wasn't much of a role model either. She left us for my father's protégé. He walked out on his wife and daughters to be with her. All for a relationship that barely outlived the media circus it created."

"How old were you?"

"A very impressionable and fragile eleven."

"She never came back?"

She shook her head. "She met a wealthy Swede who whisked her off to Europe. They had two adorable blond-haired, blue-eyed boys she named Blitz and Wagner, which between you and me always sounded like dog names. I was in high school when the rumors about her other affairs made it my way. Apparently she had quite a reputation in Washington. And there was speculation that she only married my father because she was pregnant with me."

"Is it true?"

She shrugged. "Don't know, don't want to know."

"Do you ever talk to her?"

"I get the occasional birthday or Christmas card, but I haven't physically talked to her."

"So it was just you and the senator?"

"It was mostly just me. He was never a doting father, but

after she left, he completely checked out. I had this crazy idea that if I were the perfect child, he would notice me, maybe even be proud of me. But I finally realized that no matter how high my grades were, no exemplary behavior or good deed would ever please him. He only needed me around for photo shoots or fund-raiser appearances. Anything to make him look good. Beyond that, I was either ignored or criticized. So finally I decided, why be good when being bad is so much more fun? And even better, I could make *him* look bad."

"Because bad attention is better than no attention at all," he said.

"Exactly."

"Did it work?"

"Oh, yeah, too well. The drinking and the drugs, not only did they make him mad as hell, but they had this way of making things seem better. They numbed me. Which of course turned out to be a really bad thing."

"Do you blame your father for your addictions?"

"God, no. Not at all. I'm the only one responsible for my actions. It was a bad situation, and I only made it worse. My only real regret isn't what I did to him, but all the other people who loved and cared about me. Those are the people I really hurt."

"But look at you now. You've gotten past all that."

"It's still scary sometimes, though. The idea that I might backslide, that I could let Dylan down."

"Everyone is afraid of something. If you weren't you wouldn't be human."

"I guess."

He yawned and closed his eyes.

She checked his forehead again. It felt a little cooler this time. She was about to say that she should go and let him get to sleep, but his slow, even breathing said he already was asleep.

She sat there for a few minutes more, probably longer than she should have, watching him sleep. Though it was tempting to slide into bed with him, she slept on the couch instead.

She woke to the sensation of someone poking her in the back. She figured it was Colin being goofy and thought that he must have been feeling better this morning, but when she rolled over to face him, it was Dylan standing beside the couch.

"Hi, Mommy!"

She sat up, confused and disoriented, rubbing the sleep from her eyes. "Is Colin up?"

"He sweepin'," Dylan said.

"Then how did you get out of bed?"

He looked up at her, beaming with pride. "I cwimed out. I gedda big bed now!"

Her heart slammed the wall of her chest, then sank to her toes. "Dylan Michael Tate, don't you *ever* do that again!"

The pride melted away and his lower lip began to tremble. He lowered his gaze to the carpet, fat tears pooling in his eyes, and said, "Sawee, Mommy."

She felt instantly guilty for yelling. She gathered him in her arms. "No, Mommy is sorry. I shouldn't have shouted. I'm just afraid that you'll hurt yourself."

He snuggled against her chest, so tiny and quivering. "I wanna be a big boy."

"I know you do, sweetheart, and you will be. You just have to be patient." Not an easy thing for a toddler, she knew.

"Everything okay out here?"

Rowena looked up to see Colin leaning in the doorway,

barefooted and shirtless, his jogging pants slung low on his hips.

"Cowin!" Dylan shrieked, darting across the room faster than he should have and wrapping himself around Colin's legs. Colin reached down and patted the top of his head.

"Dylan climbed out of his crib by himself this morning," Rowena told him.

"I know," Colin said, and she noticed he wasn't leaning on the wall so much as sagging against it for support. "He came in the bedroom looking for you."

"So much for our plan," she said, hoping this didn't confuse Dylan further.

"He's never climbed out of his crib before?" Colin asked.

She shook her head. "How are you feeling?"

"Like I went fifteen rounds with a prizefighter. Everything aches. Even my hair aches."

"I know! Mine did, too."

"Spare me a few ibuprofen?"

"Of course. Go get back into bed. I'll bring them to you."

Colin ruffled Dylan's hair. "You're going to have to let go, buddy."

"Dylan, honey, Colin is very sick."

"Like Mommy was?"

"That's right. And Colin took care of Mommy, so Mommy is taking care of him. Do you understand?"

He nodded enthusiastically, but there was no way to be sure if he really understood.

"Why don't you play in your bedroom for a while?"

He dutifully toddled off to his room while Rowena got Colin pills and fresh water. He was back in bed when she stepped into the bedroom, but he was sitting up. He'd dropped his pants on the floor, and the covers were pulled up to his waist.

"You slept on the couch last night?"

She sat on the edge of the mattress and gave him the pills. "Yeah."

He swallowed the pills and set the glass on the table beside the bed. "You didn't have to."

"I know."

"I feel selfish, as if I've driven you out of your own bed."

"It's okay."

"So what happened with Dylan?"

"He's been nagging me incessantly since he was two to get a big-boy bed, and apparently he ran out of patience, because now that he can climb out of his crib, I *have* to get him one."

"Why?"

"Because now that he knows he can do it, he'll keep doing it. And not only could he hurt himself, but God knows what he'll get into while I'm asleep."

"Isn't there a way you could lock him in his room?"

"I suppose I could install a baby gate. But there's still the problem of putting him in a big-boy bed. I'm so afraid he'll fall out and hurt himself."

"Don't they make little beds for smaller children?"

"Yes, they have a crib mattress that sits very low to the floor. He calls those a baby bed. He wants a twin-size mattress, but he moves around so much when he sleeps, I'm worried he'll roll right off."

"Why don't you start by putting a mattress on the floor? That way, if he falls off, he won't have very far to go. If he doesn't, then you know he's ready for a bigger bed."

He was a genius! "That's a great idea. What made you think of it?"

Colin shrugged. "It just seemed like the logical solution."

It was so logical that she couldn't believe she hadn't thought of it herself. "I'm definitely going to try that."

Colin yawned and closed his eyes.

"Tired?" she asked, and he nodded. "Did you want something to eat before Dylan and I head downstairs?"

"Downstairs?"

"It's Monday. I have to work."

"I completely forgot what day it was. And no, nothing right now, but thank you."

"On my way out I'll ask Betty to check on you occasionally, and I'm going to keep my cell phone on me, so call if you need anything."

"I will."

She started to rise and he grabbed her hand.

"Thank you," he said.

Something about the way he said it, the tone of voice, the sincerity in his eyes, made her chest feel tight. She leaned over and kissed his cheek. "Feel better."

She was almost out the door when Colin said, "Rowena?"

She turned back to him.

"I meant it when I said you're a good mum."

She tried to be. And it was nice to hear someone say it every so often. "Thanks."

She knew it was considered archaic and old-fashioned by many young women, but she had no grand career aspirations. Taking care of Dylan, being there for him, was the only "career" she needed. It was a full-time job, and one she could take great pride in. If she ever did settle down, it would be with someone who shared those values. If that man even existed.

Eleven

Colin wasn't there when Rowena got home from work at six that evening.

"Where are you?" she asked when he answered his phone.

"I'm sleeping in my suite tonight and I thought it would be best for Dylan if I wasn't there when you got home from work."

"Thanks for being so understanding."

"He's your son. He has to come first. Besides, I'm feeling better already."

"Did you eat?"

"Betty brought me a tray."

"If you need anything else, don't hesitate to call."

"I will, and thanks again."

One night before the senator came home, and then they were back to their pool house rendezvous until he went back to England.

When Rowena tucked Dylan into bed, he asked, "I gedda a big-boy bed?"

"Guess what? Mommy ordered you a big-boy bed, and it will be delivered in two days," she said, holding up two fingers.

His eyes went wide and his mouth formed a perfect O. "Not a baby bed?"

"Nope. A real bed. Two more sleeps and it will be here."

"Yeah!"

She knew that wait would probably feel like an eternity, so she told him, "You have to promise that until then you will *not* try to climb out of your crib. You could hurt yourself."

"'K, Mommy."

"You promise?"

He nodded. "Pwomise."

Despite that promise, she walked into his room the next morning to find him sitting on the floor playing with his blocks.

"I cwimed out, Mommy!" he said, excited and beaming with pride. He was just too young to grasp the danger, and since scolding him hadn't worked the first time, she didn't bother now. Before he went to bed that evening, she would take the mattress out of the crib and have him sleep on the floor for a night, until his big bed arrived. He would be safer that way. And the baby gate she'd ordered to keep him in his room would arrive this afternoon.

Dylan wasted no time telling everyone at day care about the new bed he was getting, and she had never seen him look more proud.

"So, you finally caved," Tricia said after the morning snack, while they watched the kids darting around on the playground.

Rowena told her about the crib fiasco and how she didn't have a choice. "I'm not ready for him to grow up."

"Ready or not, you can't stop it."

"I know. I wish he could be a baby forever."

"You know, you could just have another baby. Speaking of, how is Colin feeling?"

Rowena shot her a look. "That's not funny."

"Did he spend the night again?" she asked, her tone dripping with innuendo.

"He didn't. He insisted that I sleep in my own bed."

"And there wasn't room enough for two?"

"And wouldn't it have been fun explaining that one to Dylan?"

She shrugged. "Yeah, I guess I see your point. So you guys are still just having a no-strings-attached affair?"

"Yup."

"And that's enough for you?"

"Even if I wanted more than that, he's going to be gone soon."

"What if he asked you to go with him?"

"He wouldn't."

"But what if he did?"

"Relationships are really hard, and they take tons of work. And after all that, most don't even last. The last thing I want to do is get out from under my father's thumb and jump under someone else's. I just want to be…*me*. Take care of myself and Dylan. I just need to know that I can."

"It's going to be hard leaving the day care, huh? This is your baby."

Tears burned Rowena's eyes. The way they did every time she imagined leaving this place and all the amazing children she had come to love, who she had watched grow and change for almost two years. But if she was going to leave, there was no doing it halfway.

"I'm working this weekend to get the spare room all cleared out."

"If you need help, let me know."

"Won't this weekend be Colin's last weekend here?"

"That's the plan."

"So where would you rather be? With him, or cleaning with me?"

"Good point."

"You know, it's going to happen, Row. You're going to meet a man who loves and appreciates you, someone who will be an awesome father to Dylan. And you will get your happily ever after."

Rowena didn't bother telling her that fairy-tale endings didn't happen in real life.

Not in her life anyway.

Colin had a problem, and currently she was curled up against him, warm and soft and sexy with her head on his chest. It felt as if Rowena were made to fit against him, and the most disturbing part, the thing that should have had him throwing on his clothes and getting the hell out, was that it wasn't disturbing at all.

A serious romantic relationship was something he'd always gone out of his way to avoid. Not that women hadn't tried to tie him down. He just never saw the point.

Get on, get busy, get off, get out.

Crude as it might have been, it was the motto he and his mates lived by. Why would they tie themselves down to one woman when there were so many other fish in the sea? But one by one over the years, he had watched his friends begin to marry off, have families. He was the only one who seemed to be at a standstill.

"I forgot how nice it is having sex in a bed," Rowena

said. "Not that it wasn't fun doing it against a wall, or a door, or in the shower."

"Or bent over the kitchen table," he said, and felt her lips curve into a smile.

"Yeah, that was nice, too."

Colin's cell phone started to ring. He grabbed it off the bedside table to check the display. It was Rowena's father, and it was his D.C. office number.

Fantastic timing.

"Senator, hello. I figured you would be on a flight back to Los Angeles by now."

"Unfortunately I was held up. I'd like you to meet with me and several colleagues. We want to discuss forming a committee to investigate how ANS is obtaining information about private citizens, including the president, illegally. We'd like you to be a part of it, since you have some experience in these matters and that's what this treaty we're working on is all about. Can you come to D.C.?"

"Of course. But why a committee?"

"Before I can put the full weight of my office behind this treaty, I need to know the extent of the problem."

And apparently until then, he was happy to drop his trail of bread crumbs for Colin to follow. After all the work they had done, the senator still wasn't committed to the treaty? "When do you need me there?"

"We'll meet at 10:00 a.m. Thursday in my office."

"I'll be there." He hung up and tossed his phone back on the table. Damn, this was his final week with Rowena. He didn't want to waste it in D.C.

Rowena rolled onto her back and stretched, yawning so deeply that tears welled up in her eyes. "You'll be where?"

"D.C. I have a meeting with your father Thursday morning at ten."

"What for?"

He explained the committee and the reasoning behind his involvement.

"He doesn't need a committee, Colin. He knows damn well ANS is behind the hacking in the presidential scandal. He's just doing this to manipulate you, to keep you under his thumb. You'll work your butt off for him, and then he'll swoop in at the last minute and take credit."

"Probably." But Colin had no choice but to play along. Besides, he didn't care who got credit for the treaty as long as it passed. "You could come with me."

She blinked. "To Washington?"

"Why not?"

He expected an instant *no,* and she surprised the hell out of him by looking thoughtful instead.

"I do have a few things I wanted to get out of storage unit…someone I'd like to touch base with. But my father can't know."

"So we'll be sure no one knows you're there."

"Unless I have a legitimate reason to be there."

"My friend Cara is getting married. I can say that I'm in the wedding party and went with her to pick out dresses."

"And when the wedding comes around and you're not in it?"

"By then, it won't matter. And I could see if Tricia could take Dylan for the night. She's only offered about a million times. And if she can't take him overnight, I'm sure Betty would stay with him. It's short notice, but…"

He sat up and grabbed his phone, handing it to her before she had an opportunity to change her mind. "Ring her."

Not only did he think it would be good for her to get away, but he believed it would benefit Dylan, as well. Even Colin could see that he was craving independence.

She sat up beside him and took the phone. For several

seconds she just looked at it, as if she hadn't quite made up her mind, and he didn't push. Finally, she punched in the number. "Hey, Tricia, I need to ask you… What? Yes, I'm home, why?" There was a pause and she smiled. "No, I'm calling from Colin's phone. I just wondered…I mean, you've offered before, and I know it's short notice…" She winced as if she were expecting a no. "Colin has asked me to go to D.C. with him Thursday, and I wondered if there was any way you could stay with Dylan for the night."

There was another pause, and her eyes lit up. "Are you sure it's no trouble?" She laughed. "Okay, okay, I will."

She hung up and handed the phone back to Colin. "As I'm sure you've surmised, she said yes."

"Fantastic," he said, already making the arrangements in his head.

"I'll arrange for the flight. What time would you like to leave?"

"Early afternoon. That will give me time to wrap a few things before we go."

"Let's worry about the rest of it tomorrow." He pulled her down and rolled her under him. "I want to enjoy our first night in a real bed."

"But—"

He smothered her protest with a kiss, then rolled over so that she was on top, which was the best way to distract her from practically anything.

The closer they came to the end of this affair, the less he wanted it to end, yet he wasn't ready to settle down.

Rowena grabbed one of the condoms he'd left on the nightstand, tore it open with her teeth and rolled it down his erection in that slow, sexy way that she knew drove him mad. He tried to imagine what it would be like if he could never touch her again. But then she lowered herself down onto his shaft, her body squeezing him like a fist, and he decided he would worry about that some other time.

The following afternoon, Rowena said goodbye to Tricia while Colin waited in front of the day-care center in the limo he had hired.

This would be the longest she'd ever been away from Dylan, and even though she trusted Tricia, it both scared her to death and broke her heart. Dylan, on the other hand, was so excited to have Tricia stay over that he practically shoved Rowena out the door. And after going over Dylan's meds schedule half a dozen times and pointing out the emergency numbers twice, Tricia looked as though she wanted to shove her out the door, too.

"We'll be fine," Tricia assured her. "Go. Have fun, get *laid*."

Rowena shot her a look.

"Hey, at least one of us is getting some," she said. "And don't worry about me and Dylan. If there's a problem, I'll call."

The driver opened the door for her. Dressed in charcoal-gray slacks and a sweater that matched the blue of his eyes, Colin grinned as she slid in beside him, then planted one of those slow, deep, delicious kisses on her. They had a long flight ahead of them, and already she couldn't wait for it to be over so they could be alone.

"How did it go?" he asked as the driver climbed in and started the engine. "Was Dylan upset that you were leaving?"

"He couldn't get me out of there fast enough. I hate to admit it, but he'll be just fine without me. A year ago he was a clingy, needy baby who couldn't be away from me for a minute." He put his arm around her and she leaned into his shoulder. "When did he stop depending on me?"

"He still depends on you. I imagine every child his age needs a certain degree of independence. It's a good thing."

"I know that in my attempts to protect him, I've probably smothered him a little. Or maybe more than a little."

"Yet look at how capable and independent he is."

She smiled. "He is a tough kid."

Colin pressed a kiss to her forehead. "Like his mother."

She wished that were true, but she wasn't nearly as tough as he thought she was.

She looked out the window and realized they were headed in the opposite direction from LAX. "Where are we going?"

"To the airport."

"LAX is the other way."

"I booked us a flight on a private business jet."

A *private* jet? Even her father flew commercial first-class most of the time. She had just assumed that would be the case today. "Isn't that expensive?"

Colin shrugged and recited a dollar amount that flabbergasted her, but he might as well have been talking about pennies for all the concern he showed. He was so easygoing and down-to-earth, she sometimes forgot how wealthy and cultured he was. Although, come to think of it, she really didn't know how much money he had.

"You know the best part about a private plane?" he said.

"Free-flowing alcohol? Unlimited peanuts?"

He chuckled. "Those are nice perks, but I was thinking more along the lines of privacy. Meaning, no other passengers."

Well, yeah, wasn't that the point? Otherwise it wouldn't be private, would it?

"So I was curious," he said, and she recognized that teasing lilt to his tone. "Ever been a member of the mile-high club?"

She looked up at him and laughed. There was a twinkle in his eye. "Of course not!"

With one of those adorable grins, and mischief still sparkling in his eyes, he said, "Would you like to?"

Twelve

Though Rowena hated to admit it, returning to D.C. after so long felt a little bit like coming home. In the limo from the airport to the hotel, every landmark, every street, evoked a memory. Some good, some not so good, but all told, being back left her feeling not only nostalgic, but maybe even a little homesick.

Not that she would want to live there again. She'd grown too fond of the slower, less frenetic pace of Southern California living, not to mention the warmer weather. Even more crucial was that all Dylan's doctors and therapists were based in L.A., so relocating would be impractical.

That didn't mean she wouldn't mind visiting Washington occasionally, touching base with old friends. And tonight, spending time with a new one, she thought, looking over at Colin, who was gazing out the car window, his hand wrapped around hers.

When Colin made that mile-high club crack in the limo,

she had assumed he was joking, that he was only teasing her. She had assumed *wrong*.

When the jet had reached cruising altitude, the initiation into the "club" began. Since there was only so much they could do under a blanket in their seats, which in itself was probably not lost on the flight attendant, the only place to fool around was the bathroom. And for a guy who swore up and down that he'd never done it on a plane either, he sure was creative in small spaces.

For so long now her entire focus had been on Dylan and being the perfect mom. Somewhere along the way she'd completely forgotten how to have fun. How to be silly. She hadn't felt this carefree, this excited about life, about what the next day might bring, in ages. She'd forgotten it was even possible to feel this way.

In the limo from the airport to the hotel she called Tricia to check in.

"We're having a blast," her friend told her. "Dylan has been a little angel, as usual. He took an hour nap, and now we're making dinner."

Rowena almost expected to feel jealous for missing out on the fun, that Dylan didn't need her as much as she'd thought he did; instead it was a bit of a relief. She could be Dylan's mommy, yet reclaim her own identity, have a life outside of parenting. Without feeling guilty about it. Much.

They pulled up in front of the Four Seasons Hotel in Georgetown, and when the driver opened the door, a damp, icy wind greeted them, reminding her just how much she preferred the Southern California climate.

The lobby was just as she remembered. Spacious and modern, yet warm and welcoming. While Colin checked them in, she walked over to the fireplace to get warm and couldn't escape the feeling that, despite being two unattached and consenting adults, they were doing something risqué.

"Ready?" Colin asked, joining her by the fire, holding two card keys. He handed one to her and she slipped it into her purse.

"Ready," she said, feeling a bit like a princess as they walked to the elevator, his hand resting intimately against the small of her back. He was different in public. Everything in his stance, in the way he moved, demanded attention and respect. A week ago, what she would have pegged as arrogance, pretension and entitlement she now knew was confidence. He couldn't have been more polite and gracious to the staff, and when the porter met them at the door with their bags, Colin pulled out a leather billfold thick with cash and credit cards and tipped him handsomely.

The suite was ready for their arrival with a fire already blazing in the fireplace and a bottle of champagne chilling beside it—champagne that she couldn't drink. But upon closer inspection she realized that it was a bottle of nonalcoholic sparkling cider.

"I was thinking we could order room service and eat dinner in tonight," Colin said, and with a grin added, "Clothes optional, of course."

"Room service sounds nice."

"Room service it is." He shrugged out of his coat, then helped her with hers, draping them both over the back of the sofa. "Are you hungry now?"

"Famished. I was so busy getting ready to leave I skipped lunch."

"What sounds good?"

"Right now, anything." She walked over to the desk, where she figured she would find the room service menu. Through the window overlooking Pennsylvania Avenue, she could see that a light snow had begun to fall, making her grateful for their decision to stay indoors.

Cold was bad enough. Snow she could really do without.

After they studied the menu and made their choices—she tried not to look at the jaw-dropping prices—her phone rang. Her first thought was that something was wrong with Dylan, and in her mind she was already formulating the quickest possible way home. But when she saw on the display that it was Cara, she exhaled a quiet breath of pure relief.

"Sorry I didn't get back to you sooner," Cara said when Rowena answered. "Your message said you had news."

"I do. You'll never guess where I am."

"I'm guessing not California."

"D.C."

"Are you really?" she squealed, sounding so much like the schoolgirl she used to be. It was a comfort to know that not everyone had changed completely.

"We're staying at the Four Seasons."

"We? You and Dylan?"

Oops. "Um, no."

Cara was quiet, then said, "Not you and the senator."

"No, not him either." Rowena hadn't mentioned Colin to her the last time they spoke, simply because it hadn't seemed worth mentioning. She'd had no plans to start any sort of relationship with him, so what was the point? It would just be one more person to hound her about her personal life. And here she and Tricia had been right all along.

There was a long pause, and then she gasped. "Oh, my God, are you with a *man* friend?"

"I might be."

"Oh, my gosh! I'm so excited for you. Can you tell me who he is? Where you met him? What he looks like?"

Rowena laughed. "How about we meet and talk about

it tomorrow? Since I'm here, I'm going to visit my storage unit and look for that yearbook."

"I'd love to meet with you! How about an early lunch? My treat."

"Hold on a sec." She muted her phone and asked Colin, who had poured the cider and made himself comfortable on the sofa, "When is your meeting tomorrow? Because I was thinking of having lunch with an old friend."

"Ten. I'm not sure how long it will last, though."

"Maybe when you're finished, you could meet us." What was the point in having a rich, gorgeous man in her life if she couldn't show him off a little?

"Is this friend male or female?" he asked, and she could swear a hint of jealousy tinted his words. Which, she was a little ashamed to admit, she liked.

"Female."

"Sounds all right to me," he said.

She switched back to Cara. "Would eleven work for you?"

"That would be perfect."

They decided on a quiet bistro just down the street from the hotel.

"Oh, and do me a favor," Rowena said. "Don't tell anyone that I'm here. Especially my father."

"Why?"

"I'll explain tomorrow."

After she hung up, she joined Colin on the sofa to wait for the food. She cuddled up against him and he handed her a glass of cider. She couldn't recall the last time she had felt so pampered.

"Tell me about Dylan's father," he said.

The request surprised her. She turned, looking up at him, and asked, "Why?"

He shrugged. "Just curious."

"It's not something I like to talk about. The few months that I was with him were the lowest in my life."

"Dylan doesn't see him?"

She shook her head. "Dylan has never seen him."

"Why not?"

"My father offered him a big fat check and he gave up his parental rights."

"Why would the senator do that?"

"The truth is I barely knew Wiley—and yes, that's his real name. He was a drunken one-night stand that I met in a bar. Which is where he hung out a lot back then. He was a loser. A washed-up politician.

"When I found out I was pregnant it was such a shock. I was in no condition to be taking care of a kid. I couldn't even take care of myself. Then they did the ultrasound and I saw his tiny little heartbeat. It was like a sign. I just knew that I had to change, for him. I quit everything cold turkey, which was hell on earth. Cara helped me through it. It took me months to work up the courage to tell my dad. I didn't even know where Wiley was, but the senator found him and paid him to go away permanently."

"How do you feel about that?"

"On one hand I hate that Dylan will never know his real father, but on the other, Wiley was a loser, and odds were pretty good he wouldn't have been around anyway. Besides, who would want that sort of male role model for their child? In this case I think it's definitely for the best."

"What if he showed up and said he wanted to see Dylan? Said he'd turned his life around?"

"If he had truly pulled himself together and wanted to be a permanent or at least semi-permanent part of his life, I would let him. And of course it would be up to Dylan, too. As he gets older, he could get curious, or he may not want anything to do with his real father. And I have to do what's best for Dylan."

"And what's best for you," Colin said.

"Well, that part I'm still working on. But it's all coming together."

"What is?"

"I'm finally getting away from my father."

"Getting away?"

"Moving out of the mansion, getting my own place, my own job. I should have done it a long time ago, but I was so scared to screw up again. But I can't stand it anymore. When I found out what he said to you, about me being off-limits, something just…snapped. So I've been making plans ever since. Having a father in government, you would think that I would have known about all the assistance programs available, but because of the senator, I thought I wouldn't qualify."

"Why would you need assistance?"

"I blew my entire trust fund on Dylan's medical bills and now my father pays for everything. But the second I show a shred of independence he threatens to cut me off. Me and Dylan. He's even threatened to take Dylan away from me, said he could prove I was neglectful because of my addictions."

"But you've been sober for over three years. How can he do that?"

"Well, he can try, but the lawyer I talked to said he probably wouldn't get too far with it. But he can cut us off financially. Dylan's medical bills are staggering. There's no way I can afford them on my own. But there is help out there. I think it all just seemed too hard, too much to handle on my own. Maybe I didn't think I was strong enough."

He tilted her chin up so he could look in her eyes. "Rowena, you don't give yourself enough credit."

"I'm trying to. It's all really scary. But exciting, too."

He turned so he was facing her. "I think I already know the answer, but I'm going to say it anyway. If you need anything—"

"I can't. I have to figure this out on my own. But that doesn't mean I don't appreciate the offer."

"And the offer still stands. If you need anything, you can call me."

She touched his cheek, smiled up at him, and he felt an odd twisting sensation in his chest. The sudden and unexpected instinct to take care of her and keep her safe was so intense his head spun.

Room service knocked, and Colin pushed himself up off the couch to answer the door, so many different emotions knocking around inside of him, he could hardly make sense of them all.

He told the waiter to leave the tray by the door and tipped him so handsomely, the man's brows rose in surprise as he said, "*Thank you, sir.*"

With a simple gesture, he had just made the guy's day. He wished there was some way he could do the same for Rowena. He wished she would let him help her, but he understood why she couldn't. And he respected her for finally having the courage to take charge of her life. Too many people would take the easy way out.

"Well, I guess we should enjoy this while it's hot," Rowena said from behind him, but he wasn't hungry anymore.

He pulled her into his arms instead, kissed her, lifted her off her feet and carried her to the bedroom. As he laid her down on the mattress, there were no protests or bids from her to have the upper hand. She didn't try to dominate him as he undressed her and touched her. At a time when she normally couldn't restrain herself verbally if her life depended on it, she didn't say a word.

Colin whispered that she was beautiful, told her how much he wanted her, gave her pleasure time and time again, but it wasn't enough. Nothing he could do or say would ever make her see how special she was.

As he settled between her thighs, he pinned his eyes on hers and slowly thrust inside her, waves of pure emotion rising up and peaking, then crashing down over him. Skin against skin, their bodies moved in perfect rhythm. Pleasure coiled tight in his belly, pulling him under, drowning him in its inky depths. Rowena cried out and shuddered beneath him and the coil snapped, spilling over with a liquid heat that burned him from the inside out.

"Thank you," Rowena said breathlessly, clinging to him as if he were her lifeline.

He kissed her, stroked her hair, held her as she drifted off to sleep, yet it still wasn't enough. And it occurred to him, as he watched her sleep, that tonight was the first time in his life that he had truly made love to a woman.

And it bloody well was not enough.

Thirteen

Cara walked into the restaurant at 11:15 a.m. the next morning. Rowena waved to her from their table in the back, and as she approached, Cara jumped up to give her a hug.

"I'm so sorry I'm late," Cara said, giving Rowena a squeeze, then stepping back to look at her. "It's so good to actually see you in person! And you look fantastic!"

"And *you're* glowing."

Cara smiled and touched her cheek. "That's what Max keeps saying."

"He's right. You look gorgeous. Pregnancy agrees with you."

"So does having a less stressful job."

They sat down and Rowena signaled the waitress. She scurried over and took Cara's drink order, which was seltzer with lime, and they both ordered a Caesar salad, dressing on the side. Cara's with double chicken.

"Speaking of glowing," Cara said, grinning knowingly. "You're looking rather luminous yourself. Are you in love?"

Rowena smiled. She wanted to save the best for last. "We'll get to that. First, I wanted to show you this…." She pulled the yearbook out of her bag.

Cara gasped. "You found it!"

"I spent the past two hours in my storage unit digging around for it. It was literally in the very last box."

"Have you looked at it yet?"

"I didn't have time. I had to run a few boxes to the post office to ship home, then catch a cab here. I'm still all dusty from crawling around in there."

"Well, then, let's take a look," Cara said, rubbing her hands together in anticipation.

They opened the book and paged through it until they found the B's. But as they went down the line of photos, Madeline wasn't there.

Cara slumped back in her seat, perplexed. "She did exist, right? I mean, we didn't make her up in our heads."

"No, she definitely existed."

Rowena was beginning to wonder if they'd both lost it when Cara bolted upright. "Oh! I know, look after the Z's. Where they put the names of the people who weren't photographed."

They flipped all the way to the end, after Deirdre Zimmerman, and there Madeline Burch was, in the "Not Pictured" list.

"Well, shoot!" Cara sat back in a huff, then suddenly brightened. "Hey, maybe she's somewhere else in here. Did she play in any sports? Participate in any extracurricular activities? Debate Team? Drama Club?"

"I recall her being a total loner, to the point of being completely antisocial, but it can't hurt to look."

They went through the entire book, page by page, carefully skimming for anyone who even remotely resembled Madeline, which was no picnic, considering that every girl pictured was dressed in the same school uniform.

After all that searching, they came up empty. She wasn't in the yearbook anywhere.

Cara sighed. "Darn it. Looks like you came all this way for nothing."

No. She was glad she'd come. She and Colin needed this time alone.

"So," Cara said, and Rowena knew exactly what was coming next. "What's his name?"

Rowena couldn't suppress a sappy, lovesick smile. "His name is Colin Middlebury."

Cara blinked. "Oh. Would that be the Colin Middlebury who has been lobbying a certain senator to support the International Tech Treaty?"

"I didn't know you knew him."

"I know *of* him. I know that he's an earl and he's loaded. I also know that you've met men like him before. Men who needed Daddy's help."

Rowena's heart sank just a little in her chest. "He's different," she said, the protest sounding hollow and pathetic.

"How long have you been seeing him?"

Knowing exactly what Cara would think, she said, "A couple of weeks."

"So how well could you really know him?"

Cara's obvious suspicions tanked her warm, fuzzy feelings from last night. "I know what you're thinking. But it's not like that. We're not even a couple. We're just having some harmless fun."

"Oh, honey." Cara reached across the table and grabbed her hands. "I'm sorry. I didn't mean to hurt your feelings. I'm just worried about you. I know you've had it rough. I don't want to see you hurt again."

"When you meet him, you'll know he's different."

"Is he coming?"

"He should be. He's in a meeting with my father right now."

That fact had Cara looking even more suspicious. But Rowena knew she would feel differently if she met him. Not that it mattered what she thought. By the time Rowena saw her again, her fling with Colin would be long over.

Their salads were delivered and they ate in awkward silence for several minutes; then Rowena's phone chimed that she had a text message. She pulled it from her bag and checked the display. It was from Colin, saying he was held up and wouldn't make it to the restaurant, but he would see her at the hotel later.

"He can't make it," she said, shoving her phone back in her purse, hating that she could be so easily persuaded to doubt him. When it didn't even matter in the first place. They were having sex. She had no claim on him. They had never, ever agreed that it would be exclusive. For all she knew he could have another woman right here in Washington. Or maybe one in England. Or even two or three.

"Rowena, I'm sorry," Cara said. "You obviously really like the guy, and I've made you feel terrible. What do I know, anyway? I've never even met him. I'm sure he's as wonderful as you say he is."

Rowena appreciated the apology, but Cara had already burst her bubble.

When she returned to the room to find that Colin hadn't come back yet, Rowena was even more depressed.

She knew she was being ridiculous. It didn't matter what Cara thought, because she hadn't met Colin. Maybe he wasn't the settling-down type, but that didn't make him a bad person. He was a soldier, a war hero. But given Rowena's track record with men, could she blame Cara for worrying? Why would she have faith in anything Rowena said?

Or maybe it had nothing to do with Cara. Maybe the real problem was that Rowena had no faith in herself. But she was definitely working on that.

The meeting with Senator Tate was just what Colin had expected: a formality. And frankly, an enormous waste of time. He'd been subjected to a thorough grilling from the senator and his colleagues, including a top adviser to the president. But most of the questions he had no answers for, which he supposed only solidified the need for an investigation into ANS and the accusations of hacking. He was told they would discuss it further and have a decision soon. Which he knew in Washington, with all the red tape, could be months. He was disappointed, but not surprised.

As he was leaving, the senator gave him a list of nearly one hundred possible suspects he intended to investigate—*just in case.* In the cab on the way back to the hotel, Colin went over the list, surprised to find that it included everyone from aides to ANS employees to celebrities. Paranoid much? This reeked of the McCarthy hearings in the 1950s, when everyone was guilty until proven innocent, and suddenly Colin began to wonder what he'd gotten himself into. Because unlike McCarthy, Tate had years of experience and influence to legitimize his suspicions. Colin would have to tread lightly—the last thing he wanted was to become involved in was a witch hunt.

Colin was so preoccupied with his thoughts as he walked into the hotel room that he almost stepped on the thick manila envelope lying on the carpet just inside the door. He stopped and picked it up. It was sealed, and there was no writing on either side.

Could it be something Rowena had dropped?

He closed the door and shrugged out of his coat, draping it across the arm of the sofa. "Rowena, are you here?"

She stepped out of the bedroom a second later, wrapped in a towel, her skin rosy, her hair damp and a little messy.

"Hey, you're back," she said, her eager smile warming him from the inside out, and as it did, the stress of his morning, the feelings of frustration and uselessness, began to leak away.

The envelope forgotten, he crossed the room and tugged her close, circling her in his arms. Her skin was warm and soft and a little damp. She let out a soft moan of pleasure as his lips covered hers. She looped her arms around his neck and a feral-sounding grumble erupted from his throat. Every time she touched him and he put his hands on her, he wanted her even more than the last time.

"You know we have a flight to catch," she said between kisses.

"I know." He sighed and pressed his forehead to hers. If they didn't he would already have her out of that towel, himself out of his clothes and both of them back in bed.

"How was your lunch?"

"Fun. How was your meeting?"

"Not fun. More like a big, fat waste of time. They want to drag me into this congressional investigation. All I'm here for is the treaty."

"But he won't back the treaty without the investigation."

"Exactly."

"What the senator wants, the senator gets."

That was becoming infinitely more clear.

He held up the envelope. "Is this yours?"

She shook her head.

"It was on the floor by the door. I thought perhaps you had dropped it."

"Nope, not mine."

"It wasn't there when you came in?"

"Not that I noticed."

"Could someone have knocked, and maybe you didn't hear them, so they slipped it under the door?"

"It's possible, I guess. Maybe while I was in the shower."

So who did he know who would be sliding things under his hotel room door? There weren't that many people who even knew he was in town.

"Could be anthrax," she said thoughtfully, and he shot her a look. "Letter bomb?"

"Funny." He shook the envelope and something slid around inside. He felt the outline of the object and recognized the shape. "It feels like a disc. A CD or DVD."

"Why don't you open it?"

He opened the envelope and pulled out a single, unmarked CD. Puzzled, he said, "I wonder what it could be."

"Is there a note?"

He checked the envelope again and shook his head. "Nothing. Perhaps it was slid under our door in error and it belongs to someone else."

"Or it's something someone wanted you to find."

"Doesn't this sort of thing only happen in movies?"

"Colin, we're in Washington. Where do you think the ideas for those movies come from?"

In that case, if it was for him or Rowena, whoever had slipped it under the door had taken care not to be seen.

"Should we listen to it?" Rowena asked.

"I don't see why not."

He walked over to the television cabinet and slid the disc into the DVD unit, and what they heard as it started to play stunned him. The disc was most definitely for him, and it was clear why whoever left it preferred to remain anonymous.

Rowena gasped. "Is this what it sounds like?"

"I think so."

It was a recorded phone call between two men whose voices weren't familiar, and they clearly had no idea their conversation was being recorded. They were discussing plans to hire hackers to record phone and computer activity of certain relatives and old friends of Eleanor Albert.

ANS was mentioned repeatedly, and when they indicated the network's ruthless owner, Graham Boyle, by name, the hair stood up on the back of Colin's neck. Whoever put this under the door had handed Colin exactly the proof he needed to get an investigation going. And the sooner it did, the sooner he got his support.

"Do you think this is real?" Rowena asked, looking as stunned as he felt.

"I have no reason to believe it isn't. What I don't understand is why they gave it to me."

"Probably because of your work on the treaty and your connection with my father."

"And I need to get this disc to him right away." He ejected the disc and turned to her. "I think I might be taking a later flight."

Fourteen

Rowena flew back to California that afternoon. But Colin's later flight, which should have landed at 8:00 p.m., was pushed to the next afternoon when another meeting was called, and when even more evidence began to spring up in the ANS hacking scandal, he was forced to stay yet another day. And because it was pulling him away from working on the treaty, he decided to extend his stay in L.A. another week.

He swore he would be on a plane Sunday, but then he called to say that a storm had hit the entire East Coast and all planes were grounded.

Though she hated herself for doing it, Rowena turned on the Weather Channel, then opened her laptop and checked flight statuses for all the airlines. She was starting to act like a paranoid, possessive girlfriend. And all for a relationship that was never supposed to last.

He was finally able to get a flight out late Monday afternoon, but until the limo pulled up to the mansion that evening and Colin emerged, Rowena wasn't completely sure that he was coming. That he would want to come all the way back here when he could have just as easily finished his work on the treaty in Washington.

Though she wanted to run down the stairs, meet him in the foyer and throw her arms around him the instant he walked in the door, she forced herself to sit on the sofa in her suite and calmly wait while Colin dropped his things in his room, changed, then stopped by to see her. She tried to ignore the frantic flutter of her heart, the blush rising up in her cheeks. She was behaving like a giddy teenager with an adolescent crush.

The firm knock barely a minute later startled her.

Puzzled, she walked to the door and opened it. She saw a flash of dark clothing and spiky blond hair, and then Colin's arms were around her, his lips on hers, his slow, deep kiss short-circuiting her brain. And before she could stop them, her arms were around his shoulders.

Whoa, she had not expected this kind of *enthusiasm*.

Colin squeezed her tight, burying his face in her hair. "You feel so good and smell so good." He nuzzled her neck. "I didn't realize until the car pulled up in front how much I missed you."

"Really?"

He cupped her face in his hands. "No, that's a lie. I've been missing you since you left D.C."

"I missed you, too," she admitted. "I'm glad you're staying another week."

"What if another week isn't enough?"

"I guess it will just have to be."

"What if I want more?"

Confused, she asked, "More? More what?"

"More of you, more of us."

If she hadn't caught it at the last second, her jaw would have hit the floor.

And she could swear it took a full minute to wrap her mind around the concept. Then she asked the next logical question. "How much more?"

"I've never done this before, never even wanted to take next step. Hell, I'm not even sure what the next step is. I just know another week isn't going to cut it."

"Are you saying you want to date?"

"Is that crazy?" he asked, looking as if he honestly wasn't sure.

"Not crazy, but logistically I'm not sure how it's going to work, because you're not *allowed* to date me. I'm off-limits, remember? And until you have my father's full support on that treaty, you'll be taking a huge chance. If we start seeing each other in social settings, it will get back to him eventually. And what are you going to do? Move to Los Angeles?"

"I could, temporarily."

"And then what? You mentioned a security job. Where would that be?"

"My friend has offices in London and New York."

"All Dylan's doctors and therapists are here. Do you see how complicated it could be?" And all for a few more months of good sex, because when all was said and done, it would still end. "Do you see what I mean?"

He sighed and sat on the sofa. "You're right. Logistically it would be a nightmare."

"What would be even more complicated is hiding it from Dylan. He's already very attached to you. He kept mentioning you all week."

"Did he?"

"Are you ready for that kind of responsibility?"

She could see from his expression that he wasn't.

She sat down beside him. "This is why you don't date single moms. Too much baggage. And I've got more than most."

"I wish I was ready for that, or at least knew when I would be ready," he said.

"You know, I think for a while I'd like to be on my own. Completely on my own. So I'll have time to settle into independence, taking care of myself."

"You're going to do great."

She was beginning to think so, too. And though she did want to be independent, she could very easily see herself falling in love with Colin. In fact, she was probably a little in love with him already. He was the first man she'd ever met who really seemed to *get* her. But she and Dylan were a package deal. Now if Colin were to come to her and say he loved her and was ready to be a dad, that would be a different story entirely. But only if he really meant it. But she had the feeling Colin didn't say things he didn't mean.

"I forgot to tell you," he said. "I got a call today from a Hayden Black. I understand that he's a rather famous criminal investigator."

"The name does found familiar."

"Well, it seems that he's been hired to investigate the ANS hacking, and will interview the victims in Montana where the president and his ex grew up. He heard that I had an interest in the investigation and wondered if I had any information to share."

"Did you?"

"Nothing that he didn't already know. But the senator gave him the CD. It's just a relief to know that they have a professional investigator working the case. Hopefully things will move faster."

"We've had some excitement around here while you

were gone," she said. At his puzzled look, she nodded to him to follow her. "You'll see."

They walked to Dylan's room and stopped in the hall just outside. The new gate was in place in the doorway, and the light from the hall cast a dim glow inside, just enough for them to make out Dylan curled up on his new big-boy bed—a twin mattress on the floor.

"You got it," Colin whispered.

"You should have seen how excited he was. He *loves* it. He brags to everyone at day care that he's a big boy now. We went shopping and I let him pick out sheets and a comforter. Race cars, of course."

"So it's working out well?" Colin asked, slipping his arm around her shoulders.

She wished he wouldn't do things like that. It just felt so…domesticated. And he smelled so good she wanted to eat him up.

"It's perfect," she said. "I'll keep the mattress on the floor for a while and see how he does, and when he's ready we'll pick out a frame."

"You know, there's another bed across the hall that I'd like to see." He dipped his head and kissed the side of her neck. "And I wouldn't mind trying it out either. Since I'm already here."

"When will my father be home?"

He nibbled the shell of her ear. "Not until tomorrow. And if you think about it, it would be safer for me to leave in the middle of the night, when everyone is asleep."

She turned, pushing up onto her toes to kiss him, and could practically feel the neurons in her brain misfiring.

And by the sizzling grin, the hungry look in his eyes as he pulled her toward her bedroom, she had the feeling that her mattress was in for one heck of a workout.

* * *

Colin woke the next morning with the eerie feeling that someone was watching him. He opened his eyes and nearly jumped out of his skin when he saw, just inches from his face, Dylan at the side of the bed, smiling.

"Hi, Cowin!"

The clock said it was seven-thirty. *Bloody hell.* He had meant to go back to his own suite last night, but must have fallen asleep. "Hey, bud, what are you doing out of bed? And how did you get out of your room?"

"Cwimed out," he said, beaming with pride.

So much for the gate keeping him contained. If he could climb out of a crib, why not over a baby gate, as well?

Colin reached over to shake Rowena awake. "Houston, we have a problem."

She grumbled a protest, which was surely due to the fact that they had only gotten four hours of sleep, and batted his hand away.

"You *need* to wake up."

She shook her head, her hair a tousled mess, and mumbled groggily, "Too early."

"Yes, but we have *company.*"

She rubbed the sleep from her eyes, then pushed up on her elbows. "What compan…?"

She trailed off as she looked over at Colin and saw Dylan standing there. She shot up in bed as if the sheets were on fire.

"Dylan! Why aren't you in your room?"

"He climbed out," Colin said, and Dylan flashed her one of those big, radiant smiles.

"I a big boy!"

She must have decided that scolding him would be a waste of time, because she took a deep, calming breath, pasted on a tense smile and said, "You sure are, sweetie.

Why don't you go turn on the television while Mommy wakes up?"

"Okay, Mommy."

He toddled out of the room and Rowena fell back against the pillows. "Damn. Damn, damn, *damn*."

"I'm sorry, Rowena. This is all my fault. I was exhausted from the long flight and I fell asleep. I feel terrible."

"We can't keep doing this."

"I know. I'm sorry."

"From now on, we only meet in the pool house."

"Agreed. Are you angry with me?"

"This is as much my fault as it is yours. More, really. I agreed to let you stay. I figured that even if Dylan did wake up, he would be confined to his room. Worst case scenario, I would just have to sneak you out."

"Good intentions."

"Exactly. And I should get up and go check on him. And we need to get you out of here."

"First, I wanted to ask you…I know you can't officially be my date Saturday, but it might be fun to pretend we don't like one another, then try to steal a little time together."

Looking confused, she said, "I'm sorry, what's going on Saturday?"

"Your father's annual ball."

"Oh, yeah, I completely forgot about that."

"You will save a dance for me."

"I would if I was going to be there."

"You're not?"

"I'm going to be traveling."

What? She hadn't said a word to him about leaving. "Where are you going?"

"Or I might have the flu."

The flu? Didn't she just have the flu? "I'm confused."

"In light of my past behavior at his parties, I've been officially and permanently exiled from the guest list. Three years ago I was pregnant and on bed rest. The year after that I was taking care of Dylan, who had come down with a miserable cold. Last year…" She paused, nose wrinkled as she tried to recall, and then her eyes lit. "Oh, I remember. Last year I was visiting a sick friend."

"Is it any coincidence that every excuse puts you in a sympathetic light?"

"It's a silly formality. Everyone knows why I'm not there. It's been so long since I've been out in public, everyone may still think I'm an addict. Or more likely, they've forgotten all about me. At least, that's probably what the senator hopes."

"What is it that he thinks you're going to do?" Colin asked.

"I might tell a raunchy joke in mixed company, or trip on the corner of the rug and snap the heel off my shoe. I may get a little too 'friendly' with the ambassador's son on the dance floor. Or, my personal favorite, spill a double martini on the vice president."

"Sounds as if you were the life of the party."

"I was a walking, talking, sometimes slurring example of how not to conduct oneself at a formal gathering. I really don't blame him for not wanting me there."

From the other room Colin heard a knock on the suite door.

"It's probably Betty," she said. "Dylan will get it."

Colin heard the door open, then a deep voice that, unless she had started male hormone therapy, could not be Betty's. Dylan cried, "Papa! You home!"

Rowena looked over at Colin, eyes wide, and said, "Hide."

Fifteen

"Where?" Colin said in a harsh whisper.

"I don't care." Rowena jumped out of bed and yanked her robe on, frantically trying to recall if they had left anything incriminating lying around the living room. "In the bathroom, under the bed. *Anywhere*."

On her way out she closed the bedroom door. She couldn't imagine what reason her father might have for looking in her room, but she wasn't taking any chances.

He was sitting on the sofa with Dylan in his lap, who was talking animatedly about something.

"Good morning," she said, forcing a yawn. "I thought I heard the door."

"Dylan was just showing me his boo-boo. It seems to be healing well. Good thing Colin was around to help."

"It sure was, wasn't it?" she told Dylan with a smile. Then it froze like plastic on her face as her heart began to pound. *Oh, no.* What if Dylan told his papa other things about Colin, like seeing him in Mommy's bed this morning?

She'd barely completed the thought when Dylan said, "Cowin be my daddy."

"Your daddy?" her father said, shooting her a look.

"Dylan," she said, hoping she sounded calm and rational, and not as if she were about to have a coronary. "Remember what we talked about? Just because Colin fixed your boo-boo doesn't mean he's going to be your daddy."

"He sweep over!"

Damn, damn, damn. She had to think quickly. "Yes, sweetie, he's been sleeping over at Papa's house. They're working together, remember?" Before Dylan could respond, she said, "Why don't you go brush your teeth and make your bed? Then Mommy will give you your bath."

"'Kay, Mommy." He gave his papa a kiss on the cheek and toddled off to his room.

"I see that we slept in this morning," her father said with enough bite in his tone to make it clear that he disapproved.

"It's only seven-thirty."

"You don't think Dylan is a little young to be roaming around unsupervised?"

"*Roaming* around? You make him sound like a sheep."

"You know what I mean. What if he were to hurt himself?"

She was so sick of having to explain herself, as if he had ever been an attentive parent. "He woke up five minutes ago, and I was putting my robe on when you knocked."

"I'd like us to meet this week and discuss the menu for the day-care center."

"Discuss what?"

"Your snack choices."

"Is there something wrong with them?"

"They could be healthier. More whole grains, no processed sugar, skim milk."

And how about something the kids would actually like to eat?

"The last thing I need in an election year is some uptight, sign-wielding parent advocacy group targeting us for giving the kids a deficient diet."

"I've talked to you before about going organic, but you said it was too expensive."

"Then you'll just have to tighten the budget in other areas."

And wouldn't that be fun? Well, he wouldn't be her problem much longer.

"I'll have Margaret call you to set up a meeting."

"Okay."

After a few more random insults targeted mostly at her housekeeping and parenting skills—for example, if she didn't teach Dylan to pick up his toys now, he would never learn and become a spoiled brat, as she had been—he left. Why did their conversations always leave her feeling exhausted and emotionally stripped bare?

"Wow."

She turned to see Colin walking out of the bedroom wearing only the slacks he'd had on last night. "Wow what?"

"Does he always speak to you like that? In such a condescending tone?"

"It's slightly different than how he speaks to me in public, huh?"

"He addresses you like you're a child. How can you not tell him to bugger off?"

"Like I told you, he owns me."

"Correct me if I'm wrong, but wasn't slavery abolished

during the Lincoln administration? Eighteen sixty-four, I believe."

"Eighteen sixty-five. But he's a senator. The rules don't apply to him."

"There's something I want you to do," Colin said. "Something I think you need to do."

"What?"

He told her and she couldn't help laughing. "Why on earth would I do that?"

"Because everyone needs to rebel occasionally. And because it could be fun." With a grin he added, "And because the senator pissed me off, and I'd like to see him squirm."

"You don't think it would be a little immature of us?"

"Nothing wrong with being immature every now and then, either."

She couldn't deny that it might be a little fun, and the fact that her father might blow a gasket, childish as it was, was a definite perk.

"Okay," she said. "Let's do it."

At eight-thirty Saturday evening Rowena faced the mirror, studying her reflection. The dramatic makeup, the bloodred nails, the upswept do that had taken fifteen tries to get right, and last but not least, the floor-length, cap-sleeved black crepe dress that never went out of style—and still fit with the aid of a pair of Spanx.

With her painted toenails and stiletto heels—which were already mercilessly pinching her toes—the overall effect was not half bad. The rinse she'd used on her hair made it shine, and the foundation Tricia had insisted she try cast an almost ethereal glow on her face. And completely hid her freckles, which was an added bonus.

In fact, she looked pretty darned sexy, if she did say so herself. It was hard to imagine that the last time she'd worn this dress, or fixed herself up for any sort of occasion, Dylan hadn't even been a twinkle in her eye. It was astounding how much had changed since then. How much *she'd* changed.

She applied one last swipe of glossy red lipstick, took a deep breath to quiet her nerves, grabbed her handbag, then walked to the living room where Betty was watching television.

"So what do you think?" Rowena asked.

Betty turned to look at her, and her jaw dropped. "Holy canoli! Rowena, you look amazing, like a princess."

"You think so?"

"I've never seen you look more beautiful. And you're sure you want to do this?"

"Colin is right. I need to do this. I need to start asserting my independence or I'm going to wind up in a rubber room. I'm sick of feeling like my father's dirty little secret. I've been thinking about how Colin reacted when he heard the way my father talks to me. He was horrified. So I tried to hear it from his perspective, to look at it objectively."

"And what did you hear?"

"Condescension, disrespect, disappointment. I'm his daughter, and I'm sure deep down somewhere he loves me. But I've come to the conclusion that he doesn't like me very much. But you know what? I don't like him either."

"He's not an easy man to like." Betty rose to her feet and cupped Rowena's face. "You, on the other hand, are sweet and generous and kind, and stronger than you've ever given yourself credit for."

She bit her lip and sniffed. "Keep saying nice things to me and I'm going to start crying and my mascara is going to run."

Betty kissed her cheek. "I love you, honey. Have fun at the party."

"I'll try."

Trembling with nerves, she let herself out of her suite and carefully picked her way down the stairs. It had been years since she wore heels. She didn't want to make her grand reentry into society tumbling down the stairs and landing on her ass. As she descended, she looked for Colin, but he was nowhere in sight.

"Rowena!" someone said as her foot hit the marble foyer floor, and she looked up to see an old friend of her father's.

"Congressman Richards, hello," she said, offering a cheek for him to kiss. "So good to see you again."

"You look stunning. Must be that Southern California sun."

"It must be."

"Your father told us you weren't feeling well."

"I'm much better now."

"Do you remember my wife, Carole?" he said, gesturing her over.

"Of course I do," she said, air-kissing his wife, a woman she had never been very fond of. "So nice to see you."

"Rowena, you look breathtaking!" she said. "And how is that precious son of yours? He must be getting so big!"

Okay, so maybe she wasn't so bad after all. "He's wonderful, thanks for asking. He's two and a half."

"They grow so fast."

Too fast.

"Do you remember my friend Susie?" she asked, taking Rowena by the arm to introduce her.

For the next fifteen minutes or so, she was passed around from person to person. Many she knew; some were new to the senator's inner circle. And the weird thing was, everyone seemed genuinely happy to see her. There were no snickers, no whispers behind her back. She felt as if…

well…she belonged. But the one person she really wanted to see wasn't around.

The foyer and parlor were nearly filled to capacity with the senator's supporters. Politicians, actors, producers, studio execs, musicians—the royalty of California. All beautiful and exquisitely put together.

A shower of twinkling lights blanketed the parlor, and waitstaff carried trays full of gourmet appetizers and expensive champagne. Droves of guests surrounded the two bars set up at each end of the room, which she had no doubt served only the finest liquor. And it flowed freely. When it came to schmoozing his supporters, the senator spared no expense. A party like this could bring in millions for his campaign.

"Hello, *beautiful,*" someone said quietly from behind her, and her heart lifted so fast it stole her breath. She turned to Colin and it took every bit of restraint not to throw herself into his arms. In a tux that was custom fit, his hair combed and his face cleanly shaven, he looked every bit the earl that he was.

"Mr. Middlebury," she said, nodding politely, offering her hand. "You look very handsome."

He took her hand, but instead of shaking it he kissed the back, saying softly, "And you look amazing."

"I guess I clean up all right."

Suddenly the air in the room shifted, then went ice cold, as if the ghost of Rowena past had just brushed by her, and she knew without looking her father was approaching.

She took a deep breath and thought, *Okay, here we go.*

"Rowena, sweetheart, what are you doing down here?"

She turned to him. His voice was perfectly pleasant, but his eyes asked, *What the hell do think you're doing?*

"Hi, Daddy," she said in the same sticky-sweet tone he used with her, and she hoped he didn't hear the nervous waver. At least here, in front of all these people, he couldn't read her the riot act. Not that he wouldn't do it later. "I just couldn't stand the idea of missing another one of your parties."

She tried not to flinch as he kissed her cheek, and when he wrapped his hand around her forearm, the fingers digging into her flesh were a silent warning.

"Rowena, honey, you should really be in bed."

"You know, I feel just fine now," she said, gently pulling her arm back, the smile never leaving her face. "I guess I just had a headache."

"I was just telling your daughter how beautiful she looks tonight," Colin said, and for effect, Rowena shot him a look of hostility.

"As opposed to every other day when I look like a troll?"

"Rowena," the senator said.

Colin just laughed. "It's okay, senator. It's a game we play. I compliment her, and she flings barbs. It's rather entertaining."

She shot him a look that said she didn't find it entertaining in the least.

"Would you care to dance, Rowena?" Colin asked, and before she could even open her mouth to answer, her father said, "She would love to."

He said it for one reason, and one reason only, because he knew she didn't want to. Or *thought* she didn't. It was just another way to put her in her place, show her who had the upper hand.

Cutting off his nose to spite his face.

Colin held out his arm, wearing a dashing smile whose edges dripped with arrogance. "Shall we?"

She hesitantly took his arm, when in reality she couldn't

wait to touch him, to feel his arms around her. Hadn't she been looking forward to this *all* day?

He led her onto the dance floor. She tried to appear stiff and uneasy as he pulled her closer, when what she really wanted to do was melt against him, wrap her arms around his neck, pull his head down and kiss him.

He bent close to her ear and said, "You're good. Even I'm convinced you abhor me."

"I do hate stooping to his level, though, playing his game."

"Yes, but you're so good at it."

"That's kind of what scares me. I don't want to be like him."

"For what it's worth, you've left him in the dust."

"Until later when he blows a gasket."

"The question is, how do you feel now? Are you enjoying yourself? Are you happy?"

"Actually, yes, I am."

"That's all that matters, then." He glanced down at her arm, where her father's hand had been, letting a sliver of anger slip though the facade. "Your arm is red where he grabbed you."

"I'm fair-skinned. It turns red easily."

"He's a bully."

"That, too. Maybe next time I should throw my drink in his face."

"You don't drink."

"And ginger ale just doesn't have the same effect, huh?" She gazed up at him, and despite herself, she smiled. "You make me feel good."

At his raised brow, she added, "About myself."

"You should. You're an extraordinary woman. I see it. Your friends see it. The only ones who don't are you and your father. What does that tell you?"

That maybe she'd been listening to him a bit too long.

"Do you think anyone would notice if I nibbled your ear?" he asked. "Squeezed your bum?"

"Probably, but I know someplace they wouldn't."

She could tell she'd piqued his interest.

"Those doors across the room lead to the balcony. There's a dark corner at the far right, behind this enormous potted plant. Meet me there in five minutes?"

"Hell yes."

Sixteen

As they parted, Rowena nodded stiffly, as if she could barely stand to be civilized. Colin wasn't sure if her father could see or not, but she kept the charade up. What he found utterly amazing was the way men followed her with their eyes, how women burned with envy when she was close by and Rowena was clueless to it. Her self-esteem was so dragged down and beaten up, he wondered if she could ever heal, but tonight, when she told him he made her feel good about herself, he knew she was savable. And he wished he was the man who could help, who could be there for what he knew would be a very long and painful journey. But honestly, she deserved better.

And considering his recent experiences with the senator and his Jekyll-and-Hyde personality, Colin was half tempted to tell the man to get stuffed. He knew the treaty was important, but nothing shy of life or death was that important. Not important enough to pander to such an immoral, imperious son of a bitch.

But he wouldn't just be hurting his family. It would be his entire bloody country. They were the ones who wanted—and would benefit from—the treaty.

Colin walked to the bar and asked for a ginger ale. He'd sworn that as long as he was seeing Rowena, out of respect for her, he wouldn't touch a drop of alcohol. Though he was far from an alcoholic himself, it was still tough to say no when asked if he wanted a drink. He enjoyed drinking socially, although he rarely ever had enough to become intoxicated. But he couldn't imagine how hard it must have been for Rowena, especially in a setting like this when everyone he could see seemed to have a drink in their hand.

He tugged at his collar, as if he were warm, then walked out the door to the balcony. There was a chill in the air, so not many people were out there. He walked casually along the railing, looking down at the gardens below. He could see the day-care center down the hill, the back of the pool house to the right. He edged farther down until he reached the potted plant to which Rowena had referred, but it was so dark, he couldn't see if she was there or not. Then a slender arm shot out and a hand locked around his arm, pulling him behind the plant.

"Anyone see you?" Rowena asked.

"I don't think so."

"Good."

He couldn't see her face, but he could hear her smile, sense the urgency in her touch when she slid her arms around his neck and kissed him.

He set his drink down on the railing and scooped her up. With her father home tonight, they would be limited on their alone time, but he would think of something.

"I probably shouldn't mention this," she murmured against his lips, "but I'm not wearing panties."

He groaned and cupped her behind in his palms, ground

against her. They would definitely have to find somewhere to sneak off to.

"Am I interrupting something?" someone said from behind them, and they darted apart. It was clear from the voice and large outline of the individual, it was the senator.

Colin cursed under his breath.

"As a matter of fact, you are," Rowena said in a voice and a tone that Colin barely recognized as hers. "Do you mind?"

"Not again, Rowena," he said, his voice dripping with disdain.

"Senator," Colin said, stepping out into the light. Clearly the jig was up, and he refused to let him think badly of Rowena. This had been his idea, and a bad one at that. "Let me explain...."

"You just can't stop your jaws from flapping," Rowena said, and he was stunned to realize she was talking to him. "You Brits are all alike. All talk and no action." She looked down at his crotch. "No action at all. I guess some people can't hold their liquor."

What the heck was she doing? "Rowena?"

"You weren't even worth the trouble."

She started to walk away, and her father grabbed her by the wrist. "You didn't honestly think I would allow you at my party without assigning someone to keep an eye on you?"

Bloody hell. Colin hadn't anticipated that.

"I can't say I'm surprised by your behavior," her father said.

"I guess I get points for consistency."

She grabbed the ginger ale and started to walk past him, but he grabbed her upper arm. Colin saw her wince and could tell he was holding on tight.

"Should I be expecting another illegitimate grand-child?"

Colin's temper shot into the red zone and he was two seconds from belting the great Senator Tate when Rowena very calmly, and very gracefully, tossed her drink in his face.

The senator grabbed a handkerchief from his jacket pocket, sputtering and cursing under his breath, looking behind them to see if anyone had witnessed his humiliation, and unfortunately, no one had.

Rowena started to walk away, then she paused and turned back to him, saying, "In case you didn't catch it, that was a *no*."

When she was gone, the senator turned to Colin, shaking his head, wiping the ginger ale from his face. "I'm so sorry you had to witness that. As you can see, my daughter is completely out of control."

"Senator, I am—"

"You don't have to apologize. None of this is your fault. She's very manipulative."

It was finally clear to Colin what she had done. Rowena had taken all the attention off him and placed it on herself, so that the senator wouldn't blame Colin and put the treaty in peril.

"Senator, we need to talk—"

"Tomorrow, son," he said, giving Dylan's shoulder a pat as if they were mates. The fact that he called Colin *son* made him sick to his stomach. "I have guests, and I need to go upstairs and change. We'll talk tomorrow. I have some good news regarding the investigation."

Amazing how quickly the man could switch gears. How he could take his own boorish behavior, turn it around and make Rowena look like the bad guy. He truly was a master of manipulation, and Colin had reached his breaking point.

He dashed upstairs to Rowena's suite and knocked. Betty answered.

"Well, hello, Colin! How's the party?"

She didn't know? "Where is Rowena?"

Looking puzzled, she said, "Downstairs. Isn't she?"

"I'm not sure where she is. I'd assumed she would come up here."

"Did something happen?"

"She and her father had a bit of a disagreement."

Betty laid a hand over her heart. "Oh, dear."

"It ended with her father slinging accusations and Rowena tossing a glass of ginger ale in his face."

His arrogant face.

Betty's eyes went wide and she sucked in a breath. "Oh, *dear*. What could possess her to do such a thing? Although I can't deny I'm sorry I missed it."

"The senator caught us in a compromising position, and she offered herself up as sacrificial lamb to save my hide. She stormed off, and I assumed she came up here."

"I wonder where she could be. Maybe you should try her cell phone."

"Good idea." He pulled his phone out and called her, but it went straight to voice mail. Then a minute later his phone chimed that he had a text.

please ask B to watch D for the night
Thx-R

"She'd like you to watch Dylan for the night."

"Of course."

He texted back, B said ok. Where R U? we'll talk in the a.m.

He texted again asking if she was okay, but she didn't answer. He needed to talk to her. To tell her that he didn't need her protecting him. This entire mess was his fault. He had been the one to convince Rowena that she should go to the party. The one who thought it would be fun to manipulate the senator, although Rowena had been scary-good at it.

"I'm going to go get some sleep," he told Betty. Or at least try. "If you hear from her, call me immediately. I'll leave my number on the icebox."

Betty nodded, looking exhausted. "I will."

Colin went back to his suite, aware of the sounds of the party drifting up from the floors below. The senator was down there enjoying himself, spending time with his friends as if nothing had happened, while two other lives had turned upside down.

Colin finally fell asleep sometime after one. His phone woke him at eight the next morning. He hoped it would be Rowena, but it was her father.

"It looks like we're going to have to fly back to Washington and finish our work on the treaty there."

"Why?"

"Obligations. I'd like you to fly back today and meet with the committee first thing tomorrow."

Obligations? Couldn't he have come up with something more specific than that? Colin knew the real reason. The senator was trying to separate them. "I'll arrange a flight."

"Already done. A car will pick you up in an hour. I'm sending someone to help you pack."

In other words, don't let the door hit you on the way out. Just as long as he had a few minutes to straighten things out with Rowena. "I'll be ready," he told the senator. After he hung up he walked to Rowena's suite, passing Betty in the hall.

"Is she back?"

"Sorry," Betty said with an apologetic shrug. "You missed her."

"*What?* How?"

"She was only here a few minutes, just long enough to grab some clothes for her and Dylan, and all his meds."

"Did she mention where she was going?"

"Only that she's staying with a friend."

"What friend?"

Betty shrugged again. "I'm sorry, but I don't know."

He had the distinct feeling she was lying, but he didn't push her. It seemed that if there was one person who was unfailingly loyal to Rowena, it was Betty. He was walking back to his room to pack when he got an email on his phone from Rowena.

Colin,

I'm so sorry for what happened last night, and I know you probably don't understand why I did what I did, but I had to. And I can't deny that throwing that drink in his face was therapeutic. More productive than a year of counseling. I just want you to know that I don't regret it at all. I also wanted to say thank you. If it wasn't for you, I wouldn't have had the courage to do what I did. I'll always appreciate that. However, I think this is the end of the road for us. We both knew it was inevitable. But I had a really good time these past few weeks and I'll miss you. So will Dylan. Thank you for being such a bright spot in our lives, and for helping me find the courage to move on.

Fondly,

Row

He tossed his phone down on the table and it landed with a clatter.

Fondly?

She dumped him by *email* and all he got was *fondly?*

Maybe she was right. Maybe now was the best time to end it, while it was still good. Maybe now she was open to the possibility, trusted herself enough to get out and meet people, make friends. Meet a man who would give her everything Colin couldn't.

Or what if he could? What if he could be that man? What if he was ready?

He had a lot of thinking to do.

Seventeen

Rowena was in Dylan's room Monday morning packing up his toys when she heard the door to her suite open. She expected it to be Tricia with more boxes, but in the mirror on Dylan's dresser she saw her father walk in.

"Why aren't you at work?" he snapped.

Hello, Father. Great to see you, too.

Then he noticed all the sealed boxes in the corner.

"What is this?" he demanded. "What do you think you're doing?"

"Packing."

"What for?"

"Dylan and I are moving out."

"You most certainly are not."

"I most certainly am. I'm sick to death of living under your thumb, being treated like dirt. I need to take responsibility for myself and my son."

"And how do you plan to do that?" he said, so smug and self-righteous she wanted to punch him. "What will you do for money? How will you pay for Dylan's doctors and therapists? Where will you *live?*"

"I got a manager's job at a day-care facility. It doesn't pay much, and I don't have much money saved, so I'm going to stay with Tricia until I can put together a security deposit on my own place. As for Dylan's medical expenses, I'll have a low enough income that he'll qualify for public assistance. I've made arrangements to get on a payment plan with his doctors in the meantime."

"No daughter of mine will be relying on public assistance," he blustered. "I *forbid* it."

"You can't. You don't own me anymore. I was a prisoner here, and I'm free now. I'm taking control of my life."

"You don't have the slightest clue how to do that."

"I'm smarter and more capable than you think. Than you've ever given me credit for. And you've done your damnedest to keep me so beaten down emotionally and insecure that I would never realize it. So I would be stuck here."

"You and Dylan need me."

"Not as long as we have each other, and we have friends like Tricia."

"You're not fit to raise that boy on your own. I'll see that he's taken away from you."

"The family law attorney I hired doesn't think so. Well, I guess I didn't actually hire her since she was more than happy to represent me pro bono. But go ahead and file for custody. She would love it. Last time I talked to her she was already drafting her first press release."

Something in his demeanor shifted, and something that looked a little like apprehension flashed across his face. She'd had no idea that was an emotion he even possessed.

"You're not the only one with friends," she said.

"We'll discuss it when I get back from Washington," he told her.

"Dylan and I won't be here. I'm not even sure I want you to see him anymore. Not until you make some changes."

"What?" he said, sounding outraged. "I'm his grandfather. You cannot keep him from me."

"I'm his mother. I can raise him however I see fit. And I don't think you're a particularly good influence on him. I want him to learn to respect women. He won't with you around. You treat me disrespectfully in front of him. Boss me around."

"All right," he said, folding his arms. "You win. What do you want?"

"Nothing. I don't want anything."

"Everyone has a price. Do you want a larger allowance? Your own house? Credit cards with no limits? Just name it, so we can put an end to this ridiculous little game you're playing."

"I'm not sure how to say this so that you'll understand. I don't want *anything* from you. Nothing. I would rather live in a cardboard box and eat *garbage* than take another dime from you."

Her father was speechless. Did he finally realize that he had run out of options?

"Sucks, doesn't it?" she said. "Feeling so out of control. That's been my life for more than three years."

"Is that what this is? Some sort of revenge. You want to see me suffer?"

"Any suffering you brought on yourself. I've made a lot of mistakes, but I've owned up to them, apologized for them and made peace with myself. But I'm guessing that you have never apologized, or for that matter even felt guilty, for a single rotten thing you've ever done. And if you don't make peace with the people you've hurt, you're going to end up a very lonely and pathetic, angry old man with no friends and no family. And though I should probably hate you, the truth is, I just feel sorry for you."

"You'll be back," he said, but his face looked pale and there was no conviction in his words.

"Believe that if it makes you feel better," she said, pushing herself to her feet. "But don't say I didn't warn you."

Before she could make it to the door he said, "Rowena, wait."

She turned to him.

"You don't understand. You've always been so independent, so like your mother."

"And you haven't been shy about telling me that's a bad thing."

"I loved her, but that wasn't enough. She left anyway. Then you went so wild, I was always scared that I would get a phone call from a hospital or police station telling me that you were hurt, or even dead. Then you came back to me, you and Dylan... I just didn't want to lose you again."

"You're suffocating me."

"I didn't know what else to do."

"Well, then, come and see me when you figure it out. "

"But if I promise to change—"

"I need to do this. I need to be on my own for a while, just to prove to myself that I can do it."

"If you need anything—"

"I won't call you. I'll figure it out on my own."

Two days later, Colin was in Washington, working with one of the senator's attorneys on the treaty language, when his sister called. And he could tell by her tone that something was wrong.

"It's Mother," she said, her voice rough from crying.

"She had a stroke last night. She's in a coma, and they don't expect her to make it more than a day or two."

Colin cursed silently. "I'll be there as soon as I can."

He explained the situation to the senator's attorney, and on his way to the hotel to pack, he arranged for a private plane to take him to London.

The flight was long and boring, giving him too much time to think. About Rowena and Dylan, and how miserably alone he had been since she left. He had dated many women, but never had he longed for a woman, needed her deep down in his soul, the way he did Rowena. No one else even came close. He'd picked up his phone to call her at least a dozen times a day. Sometimes he even went as far as dialing, but he never let it ring. She was starting her new life, learning to be independent and take care of herself. He had no right bother her until he knew exactly what he wanted.

When he arrived in London, his mother was still hanging on, and as he walked into her room, saw her lying there looking so old and frail, he tried to conjure up an emotion—any emotion—that would make him feel as if he were losing his mother. He couldn't do it. He felt bad that she was dying—as much for Matty because she would no longer have anyone to take care of—but he didn't feel as if he was losing a significant person in his life.

Which only punctuated his feelings about the significant person he had lost. And if he let himself think about, if he acknowledged the gaping hole in his chest, he feared it would swallow him whole. And while London was the last place he wanted to be, he stayed there, round-the-clock, for Matty. They were gathered there, around their mother's bed, as she took her last shallow breath. Then she was gone. The woman who had given birth to him, but had never wanted—or even known—him. And he could only feel sad for what they might have had, but never did. That neither of them had ever really tried.

The day after the funeral he and Matty took a short walk through the drizzling rain in the park outside her flat and found an unoccupied, reasonably dry bench under a canopy of trees.

"I have to leave, Matty."

"Why?" she said, looking sad and lonely and old, and it broke his heart. It also made him realize that he didn't want to wind up like her.

"I still have work to do in Washington."

"Can't someone else do it? Why can't you just stay here in London with me? With Mother gone, who will I take care of?"

That was a lousy reason for him to stay. After only a few days with her, he'd practically gone wonky. She was so needy and clingy. What she really needed was a life of her own.

"Have you ever thought that if you went out every once in a while you might meet someone?"

She shook her head and laughed nervously, as if it were a ridiculous notion. "I'm too old for that."

"You are not that old. And I know it's scary. But you just have to put yourself out there, Matty."

"When are you coming back home?"

Home to her was London. He, on the other hand, had spent the past ten years in constant flux. Home was wherever he happened to be living at any given time.

This was the first time in his adult life that he'd even considered laying down roots. And when he thought about where home would be, he could only think of Rowena. And he realized that it wasn't about where he lived. Whether it be London or Washington or Los Angeles. *Rowena* was home to him.

"There's been a slight change of plans," he told her. "I'm going to be staying in the U.S."

She gasped, her hand rising up to cover her breaking heart. "Are you in trouble?"

"Yes and no. I'm in love." The words fell so effortlessly from his lips, he knew they had to be true. He *loved* Rowena.

"With an *American?*"

"Yes, she's American. She lives in California."

"Who is it?"

"The senator's daughter, Rowena."

Another gasp. "But…Colin…you barely *know* her."

"I don't expect you to understand. Hell, I don't even know how it happened, but I do wish that you'll be happy for me."

"Of course I'm happy. It's just that…well, the accident wasn't that long ago. You're still healing. Are you sure you've thought this through?"

In other words, she wasn't happy for him. But she would likely frown upon any life decision he made that didn't directly involve her. She wanted him for herself.

It wasn't his fault that she'd built her entire world around taking care of him, seeing that he wasn't scarred by their parents' lack of interest in anything he did. And he couldn't sacrifice his own happiness to fill the void in her life that single-mindedness had created. Not that he didn't appreciate it. But he would only end up resenting her, and then neither of them would be happy. "I've thought it through, and this is what I want."

"So it's serious?"

"Serious enough that I plan to ask her to marry me."

She sucked in a breath. "When?"

"Soon." He just needed to find her first.

"But is that what she wants, too? What if you ask and she says no?"

"Then I'll ask again. And again. I'll keep asking until she says yes."

"You always were stubborn. When you decided that you wanted something, it was impossible to change your mind. Like that dreadful motorbike you bought when you were only fourteen."

She made it sound as if he were bolting around town on a Harley. "Matty, it was a *scooter*. It barely reached fifty kilometers per hour. I was hardly in any danger. Not everyone prefers to jaunt around in a chauffeur-driven Rolls-Royce."

"I guess it's too much to hope that this woman might have even a drop of noble blood running through her veins."

He laughed. Of all the things he could look for in a woman, her ancestry didn't even make the top fifty in terms of importance. "None that I'm aware of."

"Well, if you do insist on marrying her, why can't she relocate here, to London?"

"She has a son." He explained Dylan's disabilities and the need to keep him close to his doctors. "But I'm sure she would have no objection to visiting several times a year. And you could fly to California occasionally."

"Oh…Colin, you know how I feel about flying."

Sometimes he felt as if he were *her* parent. "Matty, we've talked about this before. You have to meet me half-way."

She exhaled a long-winded sigh. "I know. I'm sorry. I'm just old and set in my ways."

"Forty-eight is not old." Or maybe it was all in the state of mind, which would put Matty somewhere up there with their mother. "I know it's difficult for you to understand, but please try to be happy for me."

When they got back to his sister's flat, he pulled out his cell phone and dialed Hayden Black, the investigator working on the hacking investigation. If he was going to talk to Rowena, he would to have to find her first.

Eighteen

Dylan sat by the television in the tiny living room of Tricia's apartment, engrossed in his Saturday-morning cartoons while Rowena, still in her pajamas, stood in the kitchen scrambling eggs in a pan with a silicone spatula. Tricia sat at the table drinking coffee and reading the paper. And though Rowena's back was to her, she could feel Tricia's gaze.

"Would you please stop staring at me."

"How do you do that?" Tricia said. "It's creepy."

Rowena looked at her over her shoulder. "When you give birth, you simultaneously grow eyes in the back of your head."

"Ew, that's just gross."

Rowena divided the eggs among three plates, then added the bacon and toast warming in the oven. "Dylan, breakfast."

"Yeah! Beckfast!" he shouted, running to the table, and she didn't scold him or tell him to slow down. Colin had been right. She didn't give her son enough credit. He just wanted to be a normal little boy, and it was wrong of her to try to hold him back, the way her father held her back. As long as he was in no imminent danger, she planned to let Dylan live his life. Experiment and have fun. To just… be a kid.

They all sat down to eat, but Rowena only pushed her breakfast around her plate. Lately food didn't hold much appeal for her.

"You know, you don't have to cook all these gourmet meals," Tricia said.

"Bacon and eggs?"

"Hey, I normally eat cold cereal."

"It's okay. I like to cook."

She was finding there were a lot of things she liked to do, normal everyday things she had been sheltered from. And now, after talking to her father, she was starting to understand why he'd behaved the way he did, why he kept her so sheltered. Even why he told Colin that she was off-limits. It wasn't some narcissistic need to control and dominate her. It all stemmed from his fear of losing her.

After she had gotten her life back on track, instead of letting her back out into the world, he'd brought the world in to her. Having Dylan's therapy there at the day-care center, insisting she live in the mansion where everything was tended to for her, meant she would rarely have to leave the estate. Even the day-care center was something he created to keep her close by.

She could only imagine what a threat Colin must have been. He had the potential to not just take her away, but thousands of *miles* away. And ironically, because she was so sheltered, so smothered by her father's insecurities, she had been that much more drawn to Colin.

The harder her father had tried to hold on to her, the more he'd pushed her away.

"Done, Mummy!" Dylan said, showing her his plate. He'd hit a growth spurt and was always hungry lately. He was still smaller than the other kids his age, but he was catching up.

"Go get dressed and make your bed," she told him. Until she could afford her own place, they were sharing Tricia's spare bedroom.

"What's with the 'mummy' thing?" Tricia asked.

"I'm not sure. He's been doing since we left the mansion. I think he may have picked it up from Colin."

"You think he misses him?"

"He has mentioned him. Maybe calling me mummy is just his way of remembering him."

"He's not the only one who misses him," Tricia said. "I heard you crying again last night."

"I think I'm just getting a cold," she said, sniffing for good measure.

"Why don't you just call him?"

"I can't. If he wants to talk, he'll have to call me."

"But it was *you* who dumped *him*. He probably thinks you don't *want* him to call."

"You can't dump someone you were never actually with."

She would never go crawling back to him. Begging him to love her. She just couldn't. Even though she loved him. Loved him with all her heart.

"I think I'll take Dylan to the park," Rowena said, getting up and dumping her breakfast in the garbage. "Want to come with?"

"Can't. I have a ton of homework."

Tricia had taken Rowena's place as manager of the senator's day care, and had also signed up for weekend and evening college classes. It would take a long time, but she was determined to get her teaching degree.

Rowena herself was loving her new job, and Dylan was

making lots of new friends. It was nice getting out every day, meeting new people. And one of the dads was clearly interested in Rowena. He was divorced, well-off and very handsome, but when he asked her out, she just couldn't work up the will to say yes.

There was also Rick, Tricia's neighbor. He was cute, but at twenty-one, too young and a little too bohemian for Rowena's taste. There was always some art fair, poetry reading or foreign film he wanted to take her to, although most of the films she'd seen lately had had animated characters in the starring roles. Eventually she would start dating, but right now she wasn't ready.

While she was in the bedroom getting dressed, Rowena heard a knock on the front door. If it was Rick, she hoped Tricia would blow him off for her. She really hated hurting people's feelings. He wasn't a bad guy. Just not the guy for her.

A minute later Tricia knocked on the bedroom door. "Someone here to see you."

Or maybe she would make Rowena do it, after all. With a sigh, she opened the bedroom door, expecting to see Rick standing in the apartment doorway. Instead it was Colin. Dylan was wrapped around his legs, hugging him.

"Look, Mummy! Cowin here!"

"I see that," she said, forcing a smile, and suddenly her heart was hammering so hard, it could have beaten out of her chest. She realized that she had been so convinced she would never see him again that she hadn't bothered preparing what she would say to him if she ever did. But this didn't mean anything. For all she knew, he could just be in town and stopping in to say a quick hello. Although she wasn't quite sure how he knew where to find her.

"Come on, Dylan," Tricia said, grabbing her backpack. "Let's go to the park."

"But I wanna see Cowin," he said with a pout.

"You can see him later. Mommy needs to talk to him alone right now."

"'Kay," he said reluctantly. "See you wayter, Cowin."

Colin smiled down at him. "You bet."

When they were gone, Colin turned to her. He looked so yummy in faded jeans and a white button-up shirt, and very rough around the edges. His hair was longer than she'd ever seen it, and it looked as if he hadn't shaved for days.

"How did you know where I was?"

"I was going to hire Hayden Black."

"The private investigator?" Wow, he must have really wanted to find her.

"But he was out of state on the hacking case. So I asked your father. I told him the truth about everything."

"Why? Why would you risk all the work you've done?"

"Because no treaty, no favor to my family, is worth losing the only woman that I've ever been in love with."

Her breath caught in her throat. "Come again?"

"I love you, Rowena."

"You do?"

"With my entire being. And believe me, I tried not to. I tried to tell myself that I would get over it, then I realized I didn't want to get over it. When I was with you I was the happiest I've ever been. And I never knew it was possible to miss someone the way I missed you and Dylan."

"You missed Dylan, too?"

"I don't know the first thing about being a good father, or even a good husband, but I want to try. And I promise to keep trying, keep working at it until I get it right."

It felt as if her mind was racing a million miles a minute. Was this really happening? Was the man she loved telling her that he loved her, too, or was it just a dream?

"Am I too late?" he said.

"No! Not at all. I love you, Colin. I've been miserable since you left."

"You couldn't have been half as miserable as I was." He took her hand and pulled her to him, and her entire being sighed with relief.

He cradled her face in his hands and kissed her gently. "I've been so worried about you, wondering if you and Dylan were okay. If you needed anything."

"To be honest, being on my own, being solely responsible for both myself and Dylan, scares the hell out of me. But I *love* it.

"I love that I have to drive to work, and that I'm paying my own bills and buying my own food. I love that when I take Dylan for a doctor's appointment, I have to stop to pay the bill on the way out. That I can make decisions about his care without consulting my father first. I like getting stuck in traffic on my way home from work, and pumping my own gas, and a million other things that most people take for granted. It makes me feel…normal."

"It sounds as if you're happy."

"I really truly am."

"Is there any room left for me?"

"Yes." She smiled up at him, touched his cheek. "Of course there is."

"So marry me."

"No."

He blinked in surprise. "No?"

"Not *no* forever, just *no* right now. I need to be on my own for a while. Besides, where would we live? I'm just getting settled. I can't leave California."

"What if I said you wouldn't have to? My friend I told you about is opening a West Coast office and he wants me to head it up."

"Where on the West Coast?"

"San Diego."

She sucked in a breath. "Seriously?"

"I already told him that I would take it. I start at the beginning of June, which should give me plenty of time to shore up the treaty."

"That's…perfect."

"So, now will you marry me?"

She shook her head. "But I will date you. Since we haven't actually tried that yet. Let's take it slow, like a normal couple."

"Would it be weird if our first official date were to pick out wedding rings?"

"A little, yes."

"But you will marry me eventually?"

"I can't see why I wouldn't."

"And I can adopt Dylan?"

She could feel tears building behind her eyes. "You'll have to ask Dylan, but I'm sure he'll say yes."

"So when can we get this dating thing going? Are you free for lunch today? And every day for the rest of your life?"

She smiled. "Let's start with today and go from there."

Their first date was lunch. Their second a movie. Their third was a day trip to San Diego. Their fourth was a trip to Disneyland with Dylan.

It was date number five when they finally looked at wedding rings, and after finding the perfect one, she finally said yes. And when Colin asked to be Dylan's daddy, he said yes, too.

* * * * *

#2215 BEGUILING THE BOSS
Rich, Rugged Ranchers
Joan Hohl

Rancher Marshall Grainger doesn't trust women...even though he's not averse to bedding them. Will a paper marriage with his live-in assistant make him change his ways?

#2216 A WEDDING SHE'LL NEVER FORGET
Daughters of Power: The Capital
Robyn Grady

When a socialite wedding planner gets amnesia, she forgets all about her previous staid, formal ways and falls for the Aussie billionaire who's her complete opposite!

#2217 ONE SECRET NIGHT
The Master Vintners
Yvonne Lindsay

Can a man who is master of all love a woman who cannot be mastered? And can he trust her to keep a family secret after their night of passion?

#2218 THE THINGS SHE SAYS
Kat Cantrell

He's her knight in shining armor driving a *muy amarillo* Ferrari. She's a small-town waitress running away. Will their passion-filled Texas road trip lead to heartbreak or happily ever after?

#2219 BEHIND PALACE DOORS
Jules Bennett

Friendship quickly turns to passion when a Greek prince and his best friend enter a marriage of convenience. But can the known playboy ever fall in love for real?

#2220 A TRAP SO TENDER
The Drummond Vow
Jennifer Lewis

James and Fiona are used to getting what they want. Each secretly plans to use the other to obtain their goal—until they make the mistake of losing their hearts.

Can one wrong turn lead to happily ever after?

2012 So You Think You Can Write winner

Kat Cantrell

presents

THE THINGS SHE SAYS

Available March 2013 from Harlequin Desire!

The only thing worse than being lost was being lost in Texas. In August.

Kris Demetrious slumped against the back of his screaming yellow Ferrari and peeled the shirt from his damp chest.

What had possessed him to drive to Dallas instead of fly?

A stall tactic, that's what.

He sighed as bright afternoon sun beat down, a thousand times hotter than it might have been if he'd been wearing a color other than black.

Just then, a dull orange pickup truck, coated with rust, drove through the center of a dirt cloud and braked on the shoulder behind the Ferrari. After a beat, the truck's door creaked open and light hit the faded logo: Big Bobby's Garage. Cracked boots appeared and *whoomped* to the ground. Out of the settling dust, a small figure emerged.

"Car problems, Chief?" she drawled as she approached.

Her Texas accent was as thick as the dust, but her voice rolled out musically. She slipped off her sunglasses, and the world skipped a beat.

The unforgiving heat, lack of road signs and the problems waiting for him in Dallas slid away.

Clear blue eyes peered up at him out of a heart-shaped face and a riot of cinnamon-colored hair curled against porcelain cheeks. She was fresh, innocent and breathtakingly beautiful. Like a living sunflower.

She eyed him. "*¿Problema con el coche, señor?*"

Kris cleared his throat. "I'm Greek, not Hispanic."

"Wow. Yes, you are, with a sexy accent and everything. Say something else," she commanded. The blue of her eyes turned sultry. "Tell me your life is meaningless without me, and you'd give a thousand fortunes to make me yours."

"Seriously?"

She laughed, a pure sound that trilled through his abdomen. A potent addition to the come-hither she radiated like perfume.

"Only if you mean it," she said. With a grin, she jerked her chin. "I'll cut you a break. You can talk about whatever you want. We don't see many fancy foreigners in these parts, but I'd be happy to check out the car. Might be an easy fix."

"It's not broken down. I'm just lost," he clarified.

"Lost, huh?" Her gaze raked over him from top to toe. "Lucky for me I found you, then."

Will Kris make it to Dallas?
Find out in
THE THINGS SHE SAYS

Available March 2013 from Harlequin Desire!

ALWAYS POWERFUL, PASSIONATE AND PROVOCATIVE.

Elite wedding planner Scarlet Anders is about to enter into a marriage of her own with the entrepreneur Daniel McNeal. Too bad she doesn't remember how she got there....

Look for

A WEDDING SHE'LL NEVER FORGET

by Robyn Grady

Available March 2013
wherever books are sold.

Daughters of Power: The Capital

In a town filled with high-stakes players,
it's these women who really rule.

Don't miss any of the books in this scandalous
new continuity from Harlequin Desire!